"It's True I've Courted Many Ladies, But Always One at a Time . . .

And you?" Robyn inquired.

"I, milord?" Pamela finally answered, striving for a playful tone to match his. "I'm a mere humble maid who spends her days baking and brewing. I haven't had time for the kind of dalliance you speak of."

"That's a great shame," Robyn said, sitting up and leaning forward. His gaze drifted over her appreciatively, and she felt an involuntary shiver move down her spine.

"As I discovered this morning," he added, his eyes half shut, "you have a warm body and a kissable mouth. A woman with such soft lips and sweet curves should be kissed often."

CLARE RICHARDS

lives in Maryland with her three children, her husband, and her tabby cat and personable German shepherd. She loves reading and traveling, and when she's not dreaming up romances she leads an active life as a teacher and nonfiction writer.

Dear Reader:

SILHOUETTE DESIRE is an exciting new line of contemporary romances from Silhouette Books. During the past year, many Silhouette readers have written in telling us what other types of stories they'd like to read from Silhouette, and we've kept these comments and suggestions in mind in developing SILHOUETTE DESIRE.

DESIREs feature all of the elements you like to see in a romance, plus a more sensual, provocative story. So if you want to experience all the excitement, passion and joy of falling in love, then SILHOUETTE DESIRE is for you.

Karen Solem
Editor-in-Chief
Silhouette Books

CLARE RICHARDS
Renaissance Summer

Silhouette Desire
Published by Silhouette Books New York
America's Publisher of Contemporary Romance

SILHOUETTE BOOKS
300 E. 42nd St., New York, N.Y. 10017

Distributed by Pocket Books

ISBN: 0-373-05202-2

First Silhouette Books printing April, 1985

10 9 8 7 6 5 4 3 2 1

1

It was only ten o'clock in the morning and already a fine perspiration had formed on Pamela Stewart's high brow. Unconscious of the picture she made with her neat profile and the wreath of dried flowers that topped her golden brown hair, the slender woman brushed back the wavy tendrils clinging to her neck. She wasn't sure whether it was the steamy late August heat or her own anxiety and excitement that was making her body temperature soar.

"Phew," she said aloud, juggling the bag of paper cups and napkins in her arms and pulling at the neck of the long-sleeved peasant blouse she wore tucked under her voluminous skirt. Her outfit was certainly a far cry from the airy little sundress the weather called for. But the discomfort of getting herself up like a medieval bakery maid seemed a small price to pay for the thrill of finally being part of Maryland's annual Renaissance Festival.

Hopping over the last rut in the dusty parking lot, Pamela broke through the screen of trees to the open meadow where the gaily colored craft booths were located. For a moment, she paused, her heart beating quickly as she watched the swirl of magicians, beggars, merchants and elaborately costumed Elizabethan lords and ladies preparing for today's press opening.

Through the thick of this happy activity, she caught glimpses of the bright yellow and green of her booth. Her chest swelled with pride. Though she'd never built anything before, earlier that week she'd managed, with the help of some of the fair's craftsmen, to nail together her stand's plywood frame, paint it and put up the banner advertising her cider and rum cakes. All she needed to do now was a bit of cleaning up and readying of her wares, and she'd be all set to go.

She was threading her way through the crowd toward the booth when a good-natured seventeenth century epithet from another part of the meadow assailed her twentieth century ears.

"Thou base knave! Thou spoonful of brains!"

Curious, Pamela veered toward a group of the fair's performers who had gathered at the edge of the woods to shout encouragement at a pair of costumed duelists rehearsing their routine.

"Hadst thou no shame?" demanded the redheaded swordsman. "Thou hast stole a kiss from mine sister. I like it not!"

"Neither did I!" returned the darker of the two with a wicked grin. The crowd cheered uproariously, and, fascinated, Pamela laughed and edged closer. She couldn't help wanting to get a better look at the tall, dark-haired, mustachioed man who continued to parry deftly the other's insults. She'd noticed him earlier that week and had admired him from a distance. And small wonder! In his high-cuffed boots and black tights, he was the picture of a dashing hero.

He and his partner were preparing to cross swords. But before they actually began to fight, they were drumming up enthusiasm for the mock battle by hurling a playful barrage of Shakespearean invective at each other. It was obvious to Pamela that they both knew well the feistier side of the Bard. They must be real actors who travel the Renaissance Festival circuit, she thought. They were much too professional—certainly neither was an amateur like herself, participating in the fair for a sorely needed change of pace.

"Why, thou damnable box of envy," the redhead spat in counterfeit rage as he whipped his sword from the scabbard at his side.

"Do you curse at me, varlet?" the dark-haired gentleman challenged with a mocking laugh, cutting the air as he drew out his own blade dramatically.

With that, the redhead lunged at his opponent. Pamela stood mesmerized. While she'd been setting up her cider stand, she'd seen the two swordsmen rehearsing and her eye had repeatedly been drawn to the chiseled features of the dark one. But here, up close, she realized that their battle was far more physical than she'd been prepared for; and when the two antagonists danced dangerously close, she started to pick up her long skirt and edge back. But just then the redhead lunged once more and caught the other man's sword, flipping it out of his sinewy hand. Playfully, the handsome raven-haired actor fell prostrate on his back at Pamela's feet. Instinctively, Pamela jumped, but before she could get out of his way, he rolled over beneath her skirts so that he was tangled in her petticoat. Pamela tensed as she felt his cheek graze her bare calf. A warm shiver crept up her spine, and to her chagrin she knew that she was blushing crimson.

"Just like you to hide beneath a woman's skirts," the redhead charged with an uproarious guffaw. "Come out from there and fight me like a man!"

From his position on the ground at her feet, the redhead's handsome opponent shot Pamela a brief, apologetic glance. "Lovely lady, I beg thy pardon!" he murmured.

A moment later he had untangled himself and scrambled up with athletic grace. Seizing his weapon, he once more engaged his opponent in energetic swordplay.

Both amused and embarrassed by her burning cheeks, Pamela hoisted the bag in her arms and hurried off to her stand. She'd been wanting to meet the man for the last few days, she admitted. But not like that. Now, after that brief contact in the field, and after the beguiling charm of his smile, she was even more aware of his attractiveness. But she was also feeling a bit foolish at her reaction.

When she reached her open-air stand, she leaned over the counter and set down her burden. Then she stood back, taking several deep breaths and composing herself for a minute while she looked up at the banner proclaiming, "Maid Pamela's Cyder and Rum Cakes."

Was this really going to work? she asked herself, unconsciously folding her arms tightly across her chest. She'd never thought of herself as the adventurous type. In the past she'd always played it safe and taken few chances. Setting up her own concession at a Renaissance Festival, of all things, seemed very daring. What if no one liked her rum cakes? What if the fair was rained out on several weekends?

Well, she told herself with a decisive nod of her head, the fair was just about to open and there was no backing out now. She'd already invested her savings in this fanciful venture and taken a short sabbatical from her job in Washington, D.C. If it wasn't a financial success, it would at least be an opportunity to put a little adventure in her life.

Just then a truck lumbered to a halt beside Pamela's stand, and she brought her attention back to business.

The vehicle, she knew, contained the gallons of apple cider she'd ordered. Right on schedule, too. She breathed a sigh of relief. When she'd first decided to operate the stand, she'd considered selling canned cider. It would have been easy and convenient. But she much preferred the taste of fresh cider and knew her customers would as well. Despite the expense of refrigeration and the need for several deliveries over the course of the festival, she felt that the better quality would be worth the effort.

When the driver went to the rear of her stand to unload, she began unpacking her bundles. But, subconsciously, she was listening to the sound of plastic bottles being stacked behind her. With each thump she couldn't help but feel a little shiver of apprehension. In a few hours she'd really be in business for herself.

Suddenly her friend Sheilah's words echoed through her mind: "You've got to be crazy!" When Pamela had confided her plans over lunch a few months ago, the blond corporate lawyer had been scornful. "Instead of doing the sensible thing and going to Bermuda on your vacation, you're going to invest your savings in selling cider and rum cakes?" At the time, the expression of dismay on Sheilah's carefully made up face had seemed almost comical.

"I know you need something to perk you up, but you don't need to stand around in the heat at some silly old fair pushing muffins," her friend had asserted brusquely. "Instead of going to work on your vacation, what you probably ought to do is have some fun, like an old-fashioned affair—you know, an out and out fling! Honestly," she had gone on, "ever since you came to Washington, you've wrapped yourself up in work. No wonder you're feeling stale. It wouldn't hurt to loosen up a bit!"

Pamela had only laughed. It was just like Sheilah to suggest a man as a form of recreational therapy. A dead-end affair, Pamela considered, was the last thing she needed. But now, as she came out of her reverie to find her gaze resting once more on the attractive swordsman in the distance who was tossing hoops back and forth with a jester, Sheilah's words came back like a recurrent tune.

"Quite a set-up," the delivery man marveled, once more interrupting her disturbing thoughts. Coming up beside her, he cast a look over the colorful meadow.

"It certainly is," Pamela agreed with a grin. "Now that you're through unloading, how about having a drink on me?" She unscrewed the top of one of the plastic jugs and poured herself and him a cup of cider. But her smile faded when she took her first sip. "Oh, no," she exclaimed looking down at her cup with a frown and then up at the trucker. "It's turned."

"Boy, you're right," he admitted after he'd taken a healthy swig himself. "Gee, I hope this is the only jug that's fermented." He shook his head. "There's been such a demand for the stuff, the supply was low when I loaded up this morning. You must have got some of the old bottles."

Pamela stared at him in alarm. "But what if everything's bad?" Visions of disappointed customers and financial ruin sprang to her mind. "You'll have to take it all back," she said decisively. "I can't sell it this way."

He only shrugged. "Some people like it hard."

Pamela's eyebrows drew together. "But it's not what I contracted for."

Grimacing, he set his empty cup down on the counter. "True. But I can't do anything about it now. I've got another delivery to make this morning." He looked at his watch. "The only thing I can do is get back to you later on. If you've got any other turned jugs, I'll replace them."

Momentarily, Pamela's mind was boggled. How in the world would she test out all those gallons of cider? If they all turned out to be hard, she'd be in no shape to drive back to her Washington, D.C. townhouse that night.

"Okay," she told him, with a sinking feeling, wondering if she was being firm enough. In her regular job as assistant grants administrator for the Harley Rutherford Foundation, she knew how to handle a grantee who didn't fulfill the requirements. But at work she had the weight of a boss and a board of directors to back her up. In this situation, she was strictly on her own. "What time will you be back?" she demanded.

"As soon as I can," was all he would reply, striding quickly to his truck and driving off.

"Terrific," Pamela commented under her breath as she turned to pick up another container to sample. "The fair hasn't even started and already I'm in trouble."

An hour later, and what seemed like an orchard's worth of apple juice in her stomach, she knew she'd never want to look at another cup of cider. However, since half the jugs she had tested had been hard, she felt somewhat lightheaded and her mood had mellowed. At least, she consoled herself, I have enough to get through today.

Setting the last of the fermented containers down, she stopped to admire the skilled juggling maneuvers of the harlequin passing by her stand. It was the same one she'd spied earlier with the handsome swordsman. Propping her elbows on the counter, she watched in fascination as three apples and an orange whizzed around in a circular motion. Then, just as the juggler moved directly in front of her, he winked and took an audacious bite out of one of the apples.

Pamela laughed in pure delight.

"My friend and I," he said, pointing to the dark-haired swashbuckler who was now flirting with the fishmonger's wife in front of the Chessboard stage,

11

"have been admiring your lovely face and wondering about you. Is this your first journey back into the seventeenth century?"

The swordsman had noticed her! Pamela thought, a little surge of excitement shooting through her. Then, smiling at the jaunty harlequin, she answered his question. "I've visited the fair many times, but this is my first year working it."

"Well, I wish you luck and a propitious beginning," he said, bowing and doffing his pointy cap.

Pamela found herself wishing she could match the man's style and way with words. Since coming to the fairgrounds to set up her booth, she'd felt a little like an outsider. This was, after all, so different from her real life, and the festival regulars were a tight-knit group. With their constant joking banter, they seemed so carefree and lighthearted, as though they inhabited a world totally apart from her normally prosaic existence. When she'd first come, she'd hoped to bridge the gap, if only for a short time. But now she wondered if that was possible.

"I'm looking forward to the next few weeks," she finally answered, noting with wry amusement that after all the hard cider she'd downed, she had to articulate carefully. "I've always loved the pomp and pageantry of the Renaissance. It's such a romantic period of history. I think working here is going to be almost like stepping back three centuries." Immediately after the words were out, she felt like a prattling schoolgirl. Her flight of fancy had probably sounded pompous and awkward.

But the harlequin smiled graciously and twirled the bell on his cap. "Well, my lady, Jake the Jester will enjoy stepping back a few centuries with you. Just remember, should you require any assistance, a gentleman to slay a fire-breathing dragon, or protect you from a churlish knave," he said, brandishing an imaginary sword, "just snap your pretty fingers and I'll be at your side." And with another courtly bow, the little jester turned and strolled down the hill to rejoin his dashing friend.

As Pamela watched his lively progress, she felt sharply how different they were. Sheilah was right, for the last few years she *had* buried herself in her work. And now that she'd just celebrated her thirtieth birthday, she was beginning to regret all those missed opportunities. With her conventional life, she was an ant scurrying around in a bureaucratic anthill, while the actors and craftspeople here were carefree butterflies. I'll never fly so free, she told herself a bit wistfully.

Forcing the disheartening thought from her mind, Pamela fished a sheet of paper from her pocket and started to check the list of things that needed doing. Though the fair would not officially open until tomorrow, everything had to be shipshape by today. After the health inspector's tour, members of the press would be making their rounds and everyone involved with the festival would be doing his or her best to impress them.

For the rest of the morning she worked hard, readying cups and napkins, and cleaning up. But despite her attempts to concentrate on her preparations, every now and then her gaze would stray across the field where there was so much distracting activity. And inevitably, as though he were a magnet, her attention would be drawn by the dark-haired swordsman.

He certainly was energetic. He seemed to be everywhere, doing everything—joining the minstrels for a song to Queen Elizabeth, juggling apples with Jake the Jester, joking with the vendors, and flirting outrageously with all the pretty girls at the other end of the field. Who was he really? Pamela wondered as she watched him sweep a courtly bow to a passing wench selling candied apples. Probably some vagabond actor who traveled the Renaissance circuit and lived the life of a gypsy, making his living on sheer wit and charm. And then she looked away quickly as his dark eyes met hers. Had he been watching her as she was watching him? she wondered. If Jake were to be believed, the swordsman had actually been admiring her.

This is ridiculous, Pamela scolded herself. I have too many things to accomplish to waste time fantasizing about a man I'll probably never meet and who wouldn't have anything in common with me anyway. Resolutely, she forced herself not to meet his gaze again. Dragging her thoughts back to the business at hand, she climbed up the stepstool to hammer an extra nail in a post that looked shaky. A half an hour later, her self-discipline paid off. For when the health inspector made his rounds, Pamela's stand passed his critical scrutiny with flying colors.

"Delicious. A+," he said, picking up and biting into one of the cranberry-apple rum cakes.

"Oh, thank you," she called after him as he turned to leave, still chewing appreciatively. Pamela sighed with relief. One test passed—though it could have been a disaster if the official had sampled the turned cider. Pamela rolled her shoulders, realizing they were tight with tension. And then she inhaled deeply three times, a calming technique she'd learned in a stress management course.

"Oh, dear," she exclaimed aloud, glancing at her watch, "the reporters ought to be arriving at any minute."

But when she looked across the field, she saw that they were already there, and the actors were busy doing their bits to entertain them. A knot of visitors surrounded the pickle merchant who had just playfully stuck a gherkin under the nose of a photographer. Yorick, the tattered professional groveler, had prostrated himself at a carefully groomed reporter's feet and was kissing her Pappagallo sandals and professing undying love. And a freckled blonde wearing a red dress was brandishing a "Rent a Wench" sign.

As Pamela took in the scene, her gaze focused once more on *her* "gentleman." He and his redheaded opponent had started another "fight" for the benefit of a group of reporters. And once more they were battling down the field, coming ever closer to her stand. It was almost like a dazzlingly fast-paced ballet, she thought, noting the graceful, fluid motions of the two men. But, as before, the dark-haired one in particular caught her eye. Despite her earlier embarrassment, she simply couldn't keep herself from watching him hungrily. Darting here and there with flashing sword, he alone was worth the price of admission, she mused.

But as the pair inched dangerously close to her booth, she involuntarily straightened up. So caught up were they in their high-spirited battle that she worried they might crash into her stand.

"Thou villain," the dark-haired fencer cried to his opponent in a resonant baritone, "there's neither honesty, nor good fellowship in thee. Fie on thee, I shall cut out thy gizzard and toast it for my supper." Grinning devilishly, he raced the last few feet up the incline that led to Pamela's concession and turned to confront his "enemy." But when the redheaded man had managed to puff his way up the hill after his fleet-footed antagonist, the latter merely thumbed his nose merrily for the benefit of his appreciative audience, who were following right along behind so as not to miss any of the action.

Pamela had backed away and was now staring with alarm at the battle raging in front of her premises. Hastily, she grabbed at some of the cups and muffins that stood in danger of being crushed. But she was too late. Before she had managed to save her wares, the dark-haired swordsman suddenly vaulted effortlessly up onto her counter, unconsciously planting one muddy boot squarely in a tray of freshly heated muffins.

"My muffins," cried Pamela, as the tray of cakes went flying in all directions.

But the rakish invader was too caught up in the heat of battle to notice the damage he'd wrought.

"A beast thou art," he tossed gaily at his baffled "enemy." Then laughing, he jumped down behind the stand and almost into Pamela's arms, which were outstretched to ward him off.

Momentarily startled by the contact with her soft, feminine body, he turned toward her. "What ho, my lady," he said, gazing down into her surprised eyes. Involuntarily, Pamela stepped backward in confusion. For the first time she was getting a clear look at his laughing face. His lean, masterfully chiseled features were a match for his ruggedly masculine body and his dark brown eyes sparkled with amusement. Despite the havoc he'd wreaked upon her stand, she felt the same magnetic pull that had drawn her earlier. For what seemed like a long moment, they studied each other, oblivious to the observing crowd. But then suddenly the stranger, remembering his audience, drew himself up and resumed his role.

And as Pamela stared up into those wickedly mischievous eyes, they began to glint with a new light. "What have we here? A beauteous maid, a damsel in distress? No," he said, playing to the audience. While she shot him a defiant look, he studied her pinkened cheeks and flashing eyes. "'Tis a distressed damsel," he corrected. "Why so downcast, fair maid?" he inquired innocently. Then, looking around, for the first time he noticed the wreckage of the muffins. "Ah, I see, I have trod where in faith I should not have," he remarked, glancing ruefully at the tray of crushed cakes that now lay strewn in the grass. For a moment a frown clouded his handsome face, and he turned back to her. "Sorry," he whispered close to her ear, "I'll make amends later." Then quickly stepping back and falling into his role, he

16

shouted after his departing opponent, "A pox on thee, Ned Quickheels! I will settle thy hash down in the glade!" Then turning toward Pamela, who still stood gaping at the audacious invader, he swooped her into his arms, and looking down at her shocked face, pronounced, "As my offending boot hath crushed thy cakes, so I shall crush thy sweet body to mine!"

Dimly, Pamela heard another cheer from the highly amused crowd as his dark head came down and his warm lips pressed themselves to hers. The kiss was as masterful and as gallant as he. As he took her in his arms, Pamela began to struggle, aware of the public spectacle they were now making. But her struggles were short-lived. In his powerful embrace, it was useless anyway. And as his lips closed warmly on hers, all her resistance seemed to melt away and she forgot the crowd of curious onlookers. Her supple curves seemed to fit against his lean muscles like a hand to a glove. As his warm mouth molded itself to hers, she felt herself leaning into him rather than pushing him away. It was as though her body had recognized its male complement. Despite everything, she gave herself up fully to the embrace, enjoying the sensations of heat that seemed to shoot through her veins.

So absorbing were these new feelings that when he finally released her, she staggered back, one hand involuntarily flying up to her mouth, as she stared searchingly up into his dark eyes.

But then she remembered the crowd, and so did he. "Farewell, my beauty. Fear not, I shall return," he declared with a mischievous smile. Once more he leaped over her counter, this time disappearing into the cheering group of reporters.

Dazedly, Pamela stared after his tall figure as it strode away in the opposite direction. Her mind was a whirl of conflicting emotions—passion, anger and perplexity eddied wildly.

She stared at what once had been her neatly ordered counter. Muddy boot marks dirtied it, and bits of squashed rum cake littered its surface.

Her efforts to make her stand a model of cleanliness had been undone in less than five high-spirited minutes. Frowning, Pamela walked to the rear of her stand, tore a sheet of paper toweling off a roll, dampened it and added liquid detergent. But as she returned to her counter, she met an apologetically smiling face. It was the harlequin-costumed juggler she'd spoken with earlier.

"Quite a mess," he commented, picking up her tray and setting it on the ledge. "Chivalry is not neat, I'm afraid." He brushed the crumbs from his hands and looked up at the agitated proprietress. "I'm sure Robyn didn't intend to wreck your pastries, but a swordsman often leaves a mess behind him. If it's not bodies littering a field, it's rum cakes crunched into the dirt," he said, waving a hand over the crumbled remains in the grass.

It was all too true, Pamela thought, surveying the damage, and she couldn't hold back a scowl. Her lips still burned from the swordsman's kiss, and her body was still tingling from his powerful embrace. His effect on her had been so overwhelming during their brief encounter that she still teetered off balance, not sure whether to be angry or intrigued.

"Who was that careless varlet?" she finally blurted out, striving unsuccessfully for a lightness she didn't feel.

The juggler smiled sympathetically. "That was Robyn O'Dare, swordsman, actor and favorite of the ladies. And a beauty like yourself," he went on, patting her hand and studying her fine-featured heart-shaped face, "would best beware."

"What do you mean?" Pamela demanded.

"Well," the jester volunteered, brushing a speck of

dirt from his bicolored costume, "Robyn O'Dare has played the reckless lover as well as swashbuckling swordsman for five summers now. He's quite accomplished in both, as you shall see. And," he added with a touch of drama in his voice, "many a damsel who's acted Juliet to his Romeo has ended up a 'star-crossed lover.' So, beware, my lady, take care. Prithee, remember Robyn O'Dare has a reputation for crushing unwary hearts as well as"—he paused, picking up a bit of trampled confection and gazing at it meaningfully—"rum cakes."

2

Even at the end of the afternoon, Jake's warning was still ringing somewhere in the back of Pamela's mind. The hours following the muffin debacle had been long, hot and tiring. All during the rest of the day, as she'd filled cups of cider for thirsty reporters, she found herself apologizing for running short of the delectable rum cakes her sign advertised. Thank heavens, at least the good cider had held out.

Now, leaning wearily against the counter, Pamela's gaze fell on the remaining crumbs crushed into the grass on the floor of her booth. It had been impossible to get them all up, and she supposed she'd be on her hands and knees picking at them until the sun set. What if they drew ants? she asked herself with a grimace. Pamela knew she was reacting out of proportion to the incident, but she couldn't seem to help herself. After the irritation of finding the cider turned, the dramatic loss of the muffins was just too much.

The realization made her cast a dark look across the

field where she could hear snatches of shouted Shakespearean lines from Robyn O'Dare and his compatriot. Even though most of the reporters and VIPs had departed and some of the booth keepers were beginning to close up, there was still a knot of cheering spectators gathered around the two exuberant actors.

Just then a light voice at her elbow made her turn sharply. "Lady Pamela, a gift for you from a most sorrowful penitent."

Pamela stared in astonishment. A pretty blond girl with a basket tray of flowers was holding out a charmingly beribboned nosegay.

"For me?" Pamela asked in disbelief.

Smiling, the girl nodded. "Yes, my lady. And it's a very special one. The gentleman who bade me give it to you asked me to explain the meaning of each pretty posy." She looked down at the colorful and unusual collection of flowers and then pointed at them one by one. "Rosemary, my lady, is for remembrance, and he wanted you to know that the doelike beauty of your eyes and the sweet softness of your lips have haunted his memory all the long day. Pansies are for thoughts," the girl went on, while Pamela gazed at her open-mouthed. "And his thoughts are dwelling on you even now. And this one," she continued, touching a yellow bloom with blue-green leaves, "is rue. Its sharp fragrance speaks of the regret it symbolizes. The gentleman who sent it is filled with remorse at his thoughtless actions earlier this day. And he begs that you forgive him."

Pamela stared down at the fragrant bouquet which she now clasped between her hands. "And the daisies?" she found herself asking.

The young girl's smile brightened. "Ah, the daisies my lady. They are the light of love!" And with that the girl turned and skipped across the field, leaving Pamela gaping after her.

Pamela held the bouquet up to her nose and inhaled its rich scent. Maybe she had misjudged Robyn, she thought, secretly relieved. Aloud, she asked herself, "Where in the world did he find pansies and daisies and rue, of all things?"

But her mind wasn't really on the question. Her gaze had strayed once more across the way where Robyn O'Dare had just completed his final performance and was taking his bows. As her eyes met his, he winked at her.

Pamela flushed despite herself. Annoyed at her reaction, she merely gave a little nod and then quickly turned away. The eye contact with the dashing swordsman had called up the memory of his kiss and the pressure of his lithe, muscular body against hers. It had been a long time since a kiss had touched her so. Though there were men she was good friends with and dated regularly, none of their kisses had left her breathless. In the last few years she had really given up on meeting the exciting knight in shining armor she'd fantasized about as a young girl. It was a shock to realize that this caress from a total stranger had aroused such strong feelings.

Once again her lips seemed to burn where his had brushed them. The seductive memory sent a warm flow through her body. And she didn't even know the man. Pamela pulled herself up sharply. She'd wanted this time at the festival to be an escape from the real world. But there was such a thing, she told herself, as leaving reality a little too far behind. After all, the flowers didn't really signify that much. It had probably been a lot easier for him to send her a bouquet than to come over, apologize in person and clean up the mess he'd created.

But it was hard to maintain that jaundiced point of view when only a few minutes later a band of seven minstrels, sent by Robyn, showed up to serenade her.

Two women and five men dressed in velvets and

bright colored silks arranged themselves in a semicircle in front of her stand. They carried a variety of archaic-looking instruments—a lute, a crumhorn, a recorder, a pitchpipe and a miniature drum. The leader, a small man decked out in bright red tights and a brown velvet doublet, stepped forward and bowed deeply to a flabbergasted Pamela.

"My lady," he began, his eyes twinkling with amusement, but his face perfectly serious, "we bring you a song from a heartsore and contrite gentleman." Then, stepping back and facing the ensemble, he blew a note on his pitchpipe, and on the downbeat motion of his hand, the singers launched into the close harmony of an Elizabethan love song.

> "It was a lover and his lass
> With a hey nonny, nonny no . . ."

As Pamela listened to the gay words, an unconscious smile spread across her features, and she clasped her slim hands. Though she was a closet romantic, her life had been an exceedingly practical affair. The only child of a widowed mother, Pamela had learned to scrimp, save and work hard to get through college. And after that she'd put all her energy into building her career. She'd never met the kind of man who could distract her from that goal. No one had ever *really* courted her—certainly nothing like what was happening right now in front of her had ever occurred before.

As the lighthearted song came to a close, she clapped enthusiastically. The minstrels bowed and curtsied after the applause, and as they turned to go, Pamela almost felt like pinching herself to see if it had really happened. Like a child who'd been taken to the circus, she'd reacted with a mixture of wonder and pleased surprise. But beneath the surface of that enchantment lurked a niggling doubt. What kind of man would put on a show like this for the benefit of a woman he didn't know? she wondered. Everything was so smooth and artful that it raised a cynical question. Clearly, Robyn O'Dare, as Jake had already warned, was no inexperienced lover. Only a polished ladies' man, she thought, a crease furrowing her forehead, could have masterminded this extravaganza of apology.

As the singers wandered off she noted that the man in question himself was now striding toward her. Pamela licked her lips nervously. Now that he was apparently going to direct more of that expertise her way, the question she asked herself was whether she could handle it. He was only fifty yards off, his dark gaze sweeping over her rakishly and a smile curving his mouth. To give herself something to do with her hands, she began furiously scrubbing the countertop with the cloth that had been clasped loosely between her fingers.

Determinedly, Pamela continued to wipe the spotless surface, her eyes pinned to her busy hands as she felt Robyn's shadow looming up. Over the edge of the countertop she could see his high-cuffed leather boots and his supple, well-muscled thighs accentuated by the clinging material of his dark tights.

Embarrassed because she'd been staring, she lifted her eyes to his face. His smile widened and his gypsy eyes laughed as he took in her confusion.

"Am I forgiven?" he asked hopefully. Even though he spoke quietly, his rich, deep voice had a resonant quality. No wonder it had carried so easily across the field.

Flustered, Pamela blurted out, "I don't know." Then, looking down at the ground, she added defensively, "You've sent me lovely flowers and serenaded me, but"—she put her hands on her hips—"there are still enough crumbs on the ground inside my stand to feed the entire ant population from here to Washington. Furthermore," she went on, aware that she was being petty but yet unable to stop herself, "I ran short of muffins long before closing."

Robyn leaned one muscled forearm on her counter and shot her an engaging grin before looking down at the ground beneath her feet. As he surveyed the damage she'd complained of, she took the opportunity to study him. There was no doubt that with his handsome, dark looks he was a remarkable male specimen. But, there was something more—an aura that seemed to surround him. He exuded a vitality that contrasted sharply with the complacency of the men Pamela worked with and had dated. Everything from the crispness of the dark hair curling at the nape of his neck, to the bronzed texture of his skin, to the small beads of perspiration on his forehead from the afternoon's exertions signaled his vibrant masculinity. And despite her strong reservations about him, she could not deny her feminine response. For a crazy moment she wanted to lace her fingers through his hair and absorb some of that electricity he seemed to generate.

But the moment passed and Robyn looked up, the deep laugh lines around his eyes crinkling. "I see what you mean and I am chagrined by my unchivalrous behavior. I can only plead that it wasn't intentional. I'm afraid I can't replace the muffins; I'm not much of a baker," he offered with a mischievous glint in his eyes. "But let me see if I can do something about the crumbs."

Before Pamela could muster an answer, he strode around the side of her stand and ducked under the railing. In the next moment he was kneeling at her feet. Pamela's mouth dropped open. Surely he wasn't going to kiss the hem of her skirt in imitation of Yorick the Groveler! Instead, he began picking the debris from her cakes out of the grass inside the booth. In acute discomfort she stared down at his bent head and lithely crouched body, and her discomfort deepened when he

announced, falling into the archaic speech of the Renaissance as though he'd been born in the seventeenth
century, "Oh, dear, crumbs do even mess thy dainty
feet, milady." His deep voice barely suppressed his
amusement. "We cannot have that!" He began to
brush at invisible spots on her slippers, his hands
coming lightly in contact with the sensitive skin of her
ankles.

That was too much. Pamela stepped back quickly.
"Oh, no, look, you really don't have to do this," she
exclaimed, making little gestures of denial with her
hands and pulling her skirt away.

Robyn looked up, his dark eyes glittering wickedly.
"Oh, but I want to. I can't rest until you let me make
amends for my ungentlemanly behavior."

"Your apology has been quite sufficient, thank you,"
Pamela told him primly. "You needn't do any more. I'm
sure by morning the ants will have carried all the
crumbs off anyhow."

To Pamela's relief, Robyn leapt up. "Oh, good," he
told her, with an easy grin. "Because, as it happens,
I've already made other arrangements in hopes of
making peace with you. And I hope you don't have
dinner plans because I'll be plunged into despair unless
you dine with me."

Ever since this rather imposing male had stood up,
Pamela had been slowly inching backward. In the
confined space of her booth, he was overwhelming,
and she wasn't sure how to deal with the charm he was
weaving around her like a potent spell. Once more she
stepped back, only to find her hips coming up against
the counter.

Placing his hands on either side of her waist on the
countertop, Robyn leaned down and looked into her
eyes. "Pretty Maid Pamela, you will have dinner with
me, won't you?"

Pamela's gaze dropped away as she struggled to

control the tingling excitement that his nearness was generating in every nerve of her body. "I don't know," she hedged a little wildly. "I haven't finished cleaning up and I'm not dressed to go to a restaurant."

Robyn looked down at her, his appreciative gaze traveling assessingly over the feminine curves beneath her long skirt and peasant blouse. The heat of the afternoon had left her damp with perspiration, and she was conscious that her blouse was clinging to her breasts. Robyn had obviously noticed that fact as well. "Don't worry about your clothes. They'll do quite well for a sunset picnic."

"A sunset picnic," Pamela repeated blankly.

Robyn nodded and then gestured behind her booth. Under a clump of tall oak trees, some of the festival people had spread a large white cloth and were busily arranging food and paper plates on it. Pamela saw that a bottle of mead sat in a wicker basket in the middle of the cloth.

"Ah, I see the royal caterers are almost ready for us," Robyn exclaimed, taking her hand in his large one.

"Wait," she said, and ducked back for her purse. When she had it in her hand, he led her toward the impromptu banquet.

Was this really happening? she asked herself as he ushered her across the carpet of grass. It was as though she were a child playing at fairy tales. This time, however, the prince was very real, she thought, glancing up at Robyn's tall form next to her.

"How in the world did you manage all this?" she finally asked, trying to regain her sense of reality.

But Robyn O'Dare didn't seem to be in the mood for mundane explanations. "Oh, a certain Renaissance chef I know here at the fair does a little catering on the side," he told her with a laugh.

"Oh," was all Pamela could think of to say as she looked down at the elegant meal spread on the grass at her feet. In addition to the mead she'd spotted earlier, there was French bread, lobster salad, cheeses, grapes, and chocolates. The sight of all that good food made her realize how hungry she was. She'd been on her feet all day with nothing but cider to sustain her. It would have been difficult to refuse Robyn's invitation before; now it was impossible.

"This looks delicious," Pamela murmured, sinking gratefully down on her knees at the spot he indicated. When she was seated with her full skirt in folds around her ankles, he arranged himself next to her and opened the sweet wine.

"They say that mead is the nectar of the gods," he proclaimed. But then, looking down at the paper cup in his hand, he shook his curly head ruefully. "I wish I could offer it to you in something a bit more elegant than this non-Elizabethan Dixie cup," he added, holding it up to the fading light.

Pamela laughed and accepted the paper container. Somehow, the little joke had put her at her ease, and she felt some of the tenseness drain out of her body.

"To a beautiful summer's end and a beautiful lady," he added, holding his cup out to touch it to hers.

Pamela smiled back at him, the sense of unreality sweeping over her again as she took in his romantic Elizabethan clothing and his rakishly handsome face with its square jaw, chiseled nose, sparkling eyes, and dark mustache. Given this fantasy setting she'd stepped into, she knew it wouldn't be hard to fall under the spell of such a man.

"By the way," he was saying, "I suppose we should introduce ourselves. Tell me, Maid Pamela, what name do you go by in real life?"

She gazed at him thoughtfully, and found herself suddenly unwilling to break the spell of their encounter by answering that question. He would probably see her as a lackluster, conventional person if she admitted that she was part of the Washington, D.C. business bureaucracy. And it was suddenly important, she realized, that he not dismiss her as being unimaginative or humdrum. Better to intrigue him as a woman of mystery. Slowly, Pamela shook her head. "I'm here to escape from the real world. Believe me, Maid Pamela's twentieth century existence is very mundane. I don't want to talk about her. In fact, I'd like to forget her completely for a time."

Robyn cocked his head. "But . . ."

Raising her hand, Pamela cut him off. "What's more, I like Robyn O'Dare just the way he is—dashing and romantic. If you tell me he's really a dentist or an accountant, everything will be spoiled." With a gleam in her eye, she raised her Dixie cup high. "I'd like to propose a second toast, milord," she said playfully. "Let's drink to escape and to fantasy."

Arrested, he gave her a quizzical look. Then he smiled broadly and lifted his glass. "To escape and fantasy, then, and we needn't bother our heads with reality at all."

Together they drank the honeyed wine, and as Robyn sipped the sweet nectar, he considered the woman before him. Since first seeing her a couple of days ago, he'd been attracted to her fresh good looks and feminine curves, which were accentuated rather than hidden by the loose peasant blouse and skirt she wore. Usually the first day of the festival he was so caught up in establishing the character he would play for the fair's six-week run, that the faces around him didn't really catch his attention. But from his first glimpse of Pamela, he'd been intrigued.

His eyes had been drawn to her as though they shared a secret. It wasn't just that she was good looking. There certainly were enough pretty women at the fair. It was a kind of glow about her. But how, he wondered, knitting his brows in puzzlement, could a woman whose eyes blazed childlike with excitement as she looked out over the fairground consider herself boring? She was the most refreshingly natural person he'd met in a long time. And she'd just refused to tell him her true name and toasted "escape and fantasy." Did that mean she was looking for a fling? Brief love affairs were commonplace in the escapist world of the fair, and he'd tasted some of those fleeting pleasures in past years. But now, studying Pamela's soft mouth and bright golden-brown eyes, he sensed a vulnerability in her. He wanted to get to know her better; indeed, he already knew he wanted to make love to her. But he didn't want to rush her and take the chance of frightening her away.

Reaching for the picnic hamper, Robyn offered her some Stilton cheese and pulled off a large hunk of French bread.

"Um, delicious," Pamela said, biting hungrily into a piece.

"Do try the Brie, too, it's excellent," Robyn told her as he filled his own plate.

He was right; it was, Pamela thought, sampling a bit of the creamy white cheese. In the fresh air everything tasted wonderful.

As they ate, they talked about the day's events: How Percy Plant, the "ratcatcher," got bravos when his rat "Alonzo" rolled over in a somersault, how Lord Dragonfire performed magic with rainbow-colored puffs of smoke. Robyn, she found, had known many of the performers from previous fairs and a tight camaraderie had been formed among the regulars on the fair circuit.

"I haven't seen you before. Have you worked any other fairs?" he asked.

Pamela paused to think out her answer. "Not Renaissance fairs," she finally hedged. "And you?"

"I've done a number of them here and in New York, though I'm not really on the circuit. But, if you're wondering how I make my living when I'm not passing the hat in crowds," he added with a twinkle, "I can tell you, without giving much away, that I'm no dentist. Are you going to make any similar admissions?"

Pamela shook her head. "No, I'd rather be a lady of mystery."

"Then I shall be a mystery man," he promised, lifting his glass.

When they finished dinner, Pamela leaned back against a tree, contentedly sipping the last of the mead. The light had begun to fade now and most of the festival workers had packed up and left for their campground further back in the woods. The field that had been so crowded earlier in the afternoon was deserted, and she and Robyn would soon be the only ones there. The thought sent a little dart of nervousness piercing through her stomach. What did Robyn really want with her? she wondered. Surely he hadn't gone to all this trouble just to apologize. No, he must have something else in mind. How would she respond if this exciting stranger were to try to make love to her? Once again she recalled her friend Sheila's words: "What you *really* need is an affair."

In Washington, D.C. Pamela had plenty of opportunities to have affairs. Over the years a number of attractive men had approached her, but somehow her relationships had never come to much. And lately she'd been feeling as though her emotions were shut down. Now, for the first time in years, she felt strongly drawn to a man. As though they had a will of their own, her eyes wandered over her companion's broad shoulders. A sweet memory of the way it had felt to be held in his arms, his body pressed close to hers, swept over her. It would be good to feel that sweetness again, even if only for a brief time.

As though something similar were running through his mind, Robyn looked up at the darkening sky. "Time for some candlelight," he announced, reaching into the hamper and extracting a wrapped package. When he'd removed the paper covering, it turned out to be two candles in hurricane lamps. "Voilà, we have light," he said, striking a match and setting the wicks ablaze.

Pamela had watched the smooth operation with a distressing mixture of anxiousness and excitement. She couldn't stop herself from commenting, "A gentleman who comes prepared with mead and candlelight is a dangerous fellow." Suddenly she remembered Jake the Jester's warning. There was no question that she found Robyn O'Dare attractive, but so had many other women, she reminded herself. And if Jake was to be believed, their reward had been broken hearts. She was already very drawn to Robyn. Could she let such a devil-may-care man as this court her without her suffering when it was all over? I'd better be careful, Pamela told herself, drawing back a bit.

"Do you treat all the ladies at the festival to this sort of a production?" she finally asked, gesturing lightly at the remnants of the picnic dinner spread around them.

Robyn gave her an amused look. "Has some varlet been filling your ears with exaggerated tales about me?"

"Well, I have heard a thing or two about your exploits with the ladies," she admitted.

Pouring himself another cup of mead, Robyn leaned easily back on his elbows, his fine masculine body stretched full length on the grass. "Don't believe everything you hear. And to answer your question, Maid Pamela of the Muffins, I'm seldom so clumsy as I was this afternoon. In my six years at the Renaissance Festival, I've never before been so boorish as to tread on a lady's confections." He paused while Pamela took in the double meaning.

She refused to be distracted by his evasive answer. "I'm told you're quite a Don Juan around here, a regular heartbreaker," she persisted, bolstered by the sweet wine she'd consumed.

Robyn paused and took another sip of wine while he

considered that. "I never break hearts, but I do try to get them beating a little faster; which, after all, is good for the circulation." He winked at her unabashedly and then continued. "I'm certainly not a Don Juan, I hope. I see myself as having a bit more class, like a Sir Walter Raleigh spreading his cape over a mud puddle to keep a lady's feet dry. Or a Lord Essex risking his life to bring pirate gold home to his Lady Fair."

"You mean 'ladies fair,' don't you?" Pamela corrected.

Robyn threw back his head and laughed. "It's true I've courted many ladies, but always one at a time. Juggling is not my specialty. And you?" he inquired.

Despite their earlier agreement, he seemed intensely curious about her, Pamela thought. She'd been parrying his adroit attempts to elicit information all evening. But there was no way she could answer this query without revealing more than she wanted to about herself.

"I, milord?" she finally answered, striving for a playful tone to match his. "I'm a mere humble maid who spends her days baking and brewing. I haven't had time for the kind of dalliance you speak of."

"That's a great shame," Robyn said, sitting up and leaning forward. His gaze drifted over her appreciatively, and she felt an involuntary shiver move down her spine.

"As I discovered this morning," he added, his eyes half shut, "you have a warm body and a kissable mouth. A woman with such soft lips and sweet curves should be kissed often." His hand reached up and touched her chin, turning her face up to his, and Pamela's breath seemed to stop in her chest. She knew he was going to kiss her now. If she were wise, she'd draw back, but she wanted to feel the touch of his mouth on hers again. Her body's needs and wants seemed to block the warnings her brain was sending.

Around them the fairground itself was now deserted. But, after all, what harm could one more kiss do? As Robyn's lips descended on hers, Pamela knew she was rationalizing. But when their mouths touched and melded, all thought fled.

When this swashbuckling charmer had kissed her before, she'd been so caught off balance that she hadn't been able to take in the experience fully. But now all her senses were alive to the sensations his closeness was evoking. As he wrapped his arms around her shoulders and drew her against him, her hands went out. The powerful circle of his embrace tightened, and her fingers touched the open neck of the cambric shirt beneath his leather tunic. The fine texture of the linen contrasted with the roughness of the chest hair escaping the shirt's vee neck. Her fingers slipped beneath the smooth material, feeling his muscular chest and twining through the curly strands that covered it.

As his lips explored the line of her mouth, she absorbed not only the feel, but the scent of him. There was a healthy masculine fragrance about him accentuated by the exertions of the day. That, mixed with the rich leather smell of his tunic, struck at Pamela's senses in a heady, erotic blend.

Slowly, Robyn's hands moved down the line of her back, awakening all the nerve ends he found there. Involuntarily, Pamela moved closer, molding her body to his. So absorbed was she in the sensations he was arousing that she barely noticed when he began gently lowering her to the ground. As he stretched her out, his mouth moved from her lips to the line of her jaw, to the delicate skin of her neck and throat.

"You're beautiful," he murmured into her ear before his teeth found her lobe and nipped gently. "You taste even sweeter than your rum cakes."

A tremor of desire shot through Pamela's system. Robyn's honeyed words and sensual caresses were awakening needs and feelings she'd never been aware of. The strength of her reaction was a bit frightening, and for a moment she almost drew back. But then Robyn's hand cupped the full curve of her breast. Little quivers of heated excitement shot through her, and her protest died before it was born.

This was a man who knew how to make her body respond as a master musician might a fine stringed instrument. She knew she should be put off by his expertise, but she was too caught up in her passion for that.

"All day, I've thought of nothing but this," Robyn whispered, his breath warm against her cheek. He had lowered his body onto hers, and propping his elbows on either side of her, he looked down into her face. "Sweet Lady, dost thou forgive me for trampling on your muffins?" he asked in a teasing tone while he ran long tanned fingers along the high line of her cheekbone. "I think we were fated to meet like this. I do believe Fortune herself preordained that I step where I shouldn't."

Pamela looked up. Robyn's black eyes were sparkling like polished jet. Suddenly a vague suspicion swept through her mind. She narrowed her eyes slightly. "You devil," she accused, breaking into a smile and giving him a playful shove. "Are you sure you didn't plan that?"

Sitting up, Robyn raised his hands palms upward in mock outrage. "Milady, dost thou think for one moment that I would stoop to such a scandalous ploy?"

"You . . . you . . . miscreant, you didn't, did you?"

He shook his head and stretched out next to her again. "No, Pamela, it wasn't planned." Then he grinned like a mischievous boy. "However," he said, holding up one finger, "I'll have to keep it in mind for future reference. It wasn't such a bad device, was it?" They both laughed. "It *was* fate," Robyn repeated. And then his arms were around her, and his mouth came to explore hers once more.

Darkness had begun to shroud the deserted field and the moon and stars were faintly visible in the lavender-streaked sky. As Robyn covered her face with drugging kisses, Pamela was only faintly aware of the onset of the rhythmic serenade of chorusing crickets. She opened her eyes to look dazedly up at his shadowy features. His eyes no longer held the teasing glint that had charmed her earlier. Now his expression was intent, and all at once she was aware of the hard imprint of his aroused masculinity pressed against her hip.

It was then that she felt Robyn's hand slide beneath her skirt and touch her naked thigh. The contact was electrifying. Desperately, Pamela struggled to rouse herself from the sensual haze she'd drifted into. Her body wanted what he was doing. There was no question about that. But, a warning voice from within her scolded, did *she?*

He was a stranger, a man she'd only known for a few hours, who had mesmerized her with his flamboyant charm. How could he see her as anything but an amusing yet meaningless interlude? And that, no matter how much she wanted to escape the routine of her life, was not the way she would ever want to think of herself. What was more, she would be seeing him repeatedly as long as the festival ran. Undoubtedly, he would be flirting with and making love to other women during that time. Being part of a temporary harem definitely did not appeal to her.

But even as these thoughts echoed through her head, she couldn't curb the response he was drawing from her. Her hips undulated in age-old invitation, and her lips clung to his. Little flames burst into life in her veins.

Just at that moment there was a swift movement in the woods. Pamela's heart jerked. As though someone had rung a firebell in her ear, she pushed Robyn away, sat up and smoothed down her skirt.

"What's wrong?" he demanded, reaching for her again.

But she put out her hands to stop him. "I heard someone in the woods."

Robyn leaned forward to nibble on her ear. "Probably only an animal."

He was undoubtedly right, Pamela acknowledged. But now that she'd come to her senses, she was going to seize on the excuse to stop before she made a complete fool of herself.

"No." She flattened her palms against his broad chest and pushed him away. "I have to leave now."

Robyn drew back and stared at her in disbelief. "You can't be serious!"

"Oh, I'm very serious," she replied, scrambling to her feet and brushing the grass from her skirt. "Thank you for the lovely dinner. You've more than made up for ruining my cakes."

Slowly Robyn rose to his feet, a quizzical expression on his handsome face. "I'm sorry, Pamela. I didn't mean to rush you." He shook his head ruefully. "I'm beginning to make a career of apologizing to you," he went on with a self-deprecating laugh.

Pamela felt her cheeks redden. Thank goodness it was too dark for him to see. Businesslike, she thrust out her hand. "No, this time it was my fault, not just yours. Perhaps we'll see each other again, but right now I have to get home." And with that, she picked up her purse, lifted her skirts, and dashed toward the parking lot, while Robyn stared after her.

3

The tantalizing fragrance of baking muffins permeated Pamela's sunny kitchen. Dressed in worn jeans and a teal blue tee-shirt, her hair pinned up in braids, she was bent intently over an enormous crockery mixing bowl. It was a farm antique that she'd picked up at an auction along with the old freezer in the basement that was now almost completely filled with her rum cakes.

As she beat the batter, she hummed "Greensleeves," one of her favorite songs and a frequently heard tune at the Renaissance Festival. Glancing up at the clock, she noted that it was 10:00 A.M. She'd only been working since nine o'clock and already her arms ached. Thinking of the batch of muffins she had yet to mix up, she reflected, By the time the festival's over, I'll look like I had a course at Nautilus.

Thoughts of the festival in general and Robyn O'Dare in particular had been occupying her mind all week. Since that romantic Sunday evening picnic when she'd fled his arms, she'd been alternately shocked by her abandoned behavior and regretful that she hadn't stayed with the intriguing actor a bit longer. After all, when would she ever again have the opportunity to taste the kisses of such an exciting male? But gradually, as the days passed, she'd regained her sense of balance. She had no intention of hurling herself headlong into the arms of a man she barely knew—no matter how romantically appealing he was.

Absentmindedly, Pamela rubbed the back of her hand along the line of her cheek, leaving a dusting of flour behind. The little she did know of Robyn O'Dare, she warned herself, made it clear they were completely unsuited. He was a vagabond actor with a devil-may-care attitude toward life and, undoubtedly, toward women as well. Like the tale in Aesop's fables, he was the carefree grasshopper, and she was the industrious ant. Pamela smiled wryly. Clearly, they were different species. Thank goodness she'd only be exposed to his magnetism during the festival weekends. It would take at least a week to recover from the heady intoxication of his personality.

The timer went off and, wiping her hands on her apron, Pamela thrust her hands into padded mitts and withdrew her second batch of muffins from the oven. While they cooled, she ladled batter into another tin and popped it in to bake. She was just about to assemble the ingredients for her last batch, when, to her surprise, the front doorbell chimed.

Who would that be? she wondered, circling through the hall that led to the small foyer with its off-white, patterned ceramic tile floor and subtly flowered Williamsburg wallpaper.

"Coming," she sang out as the bell rang again. Years of living in a big city had taught her caution, and before opening the door she paused to peer through the peephole. What she saw made her freeze. The tall, lean body on the other side didn't belong to her neighbor Mrs. Snow, or the paperboy.

"Robyn O'Dare," she whispered, a tingle of excitement rippling through her. Quickly, she turned toward the ornately framed mirror in the hallway and glanced anxiously at her reflection. What she saw was not encouraging, for she hadn't bothered with makeup that morning. There was flour on her face, and wisps of hair had escaped her braids. But there wasn't much she could do about her appearance now, she realized as the doorbell sounded again. Brushing the flour from her cheek and patting her hair ineffectually, she muttered, "Oh, my God," and turned back to the door to open it.

"Maid Muffin!" the tall man on her front steps exclaimed with a graceful bow. They were standing face to face, and while he grinned down at her disheveled appearance, she gaped up at him. He looked entirely different. The colorful Renaissance attire that she remembered so vividly was gone, and in its place was a pair of snug jeans and a white knit shirt. Unexpectedly, the casual outfit suited him well. The faded denim clung attractively to his narrow hips and muscular thighs. And the knit top stretched tautly across his broad chest, hinting at the strength beneath. He was still smiling at her, and the white of the shirt matched his sparkling teeth, setting off the bronze of his darkly handsome face.

The man's physical impact was simply dazzling, Pamela acknowledged to herself. Once again, despite all her reservations, she found herself succumbing to his appeal and smiling back at him with a slightly dazed expression in her golden brown eyes.

"You see," he was saying in an amused baritone, "there's no escaping me. I've tracked you down."

"How? . . . where?" Pamela stammered.

"It's my army of spies," he went on, lifting one black eyebrow in amusement. Then, with a little flourish, he pulled a bottle out of the bag he held in his left arm. "Last Sunday, after our picnic, you ran away so quickly that I didn't get a chance to properly apologize for coming on so strong. So I've brought a peace offering of champagne and strawberries."

Pamela stared at the gift he was proffering, her mind a blank. "Champagne and strawberries," she repeated stupidly.

"I think it's time we stepped out of our roles at the festival and into the twentieth century, so we can get to know each other properly," he explained. "May I come in?"

"Of course." Hastily, she stepped aside so that he could walk past her. Pamela was still so startled by his unexpected appearance that she was finding it difficult to think. As she led him into the kitchen, she began to make apologies for herself.

"Sorry about the mess. I was baking this morning, and I wasn't expecting company." She looked ruefully down at her jeans.

Robyn smiled warmly at her, then sniffed the air and glanced appreciatively at the trays of cooling cakes. "Don't worry about it. You look almost as delicious as your kitchen smells." Still offering her his beguiling smile, he picked up a muffin, inhaled as though it were ambrosia, and then took a bite and chewed with relish. "I much prefer these without my footprints on them," he said, winking mischievously.

Pamela couldn't stop herself from laughing at his impudent reference to their first disastrous encounter. "Me too," she allowed.

"Ah, at least we agree on something. Let's go on from there." He finished off the muffin and leaned comfortably against the kitchen counter. "First things first. I know, when last we met, we agreed to keep our identities mysterious, but I think it's time we removed our masks, so to speak."

He paused to glance questioningly at her. But Pamela could think of nothing to say. Once again, she felt as if she were being mesmerized by this compelling man. It was frightening how easily he was able to cast a spell over her. When she made no answer, he continued.

"I am not an accountant, by the way, and I've already told you I'm not a dentist. You aren't by any chance a dentist, are you?" he teased.

Quickly, Pamela shook her head. "No, not even a dental hygienist."

He grinned, an expression which, on his face, was as devastating to Pamela's composure as exploding dynamite is to loose rock.

"Then we're on safe ground. I'd like to formally introduce myself," he went on with a little mock bow. "I'm Robert Darcy; my friends call me Rob. And you're Pamela Stewart."

When she looked surprised, he added, "I know because I did some research."

"Research?"

He chuckled. "Yes, I talked to the festival's director."

Pamela gave a little laugh. Then, putting a hand on her hip and cocking her head, she said, "One of your spies, no doubt."

"No doubt." His eyebrows lifted melodramatically. "They're everywhere." He looked around at the cooling muffins and dirty pans. Then, gesturing at the champagne, he asked, "Are you ready for a brunch break?"

Just then the timer went off again. Grabbing her mitts, Pamela rescued the cakes from the oven and a new wave of cranberry and apple aroma filled the kitchen. Then, after glancing up at the clock on the wall, she turned back to Rob. The interruption had given her time to collect herself and remember her plans for the morning.

"Well, I'd really like to get a few more muffins baked before stopping." She gestured at her worktable. "I was just about to mix up some more batter when you came."

Rob seemed undaunted. "Then let me help." Grabbing the measuring cup, he held it aloft. "Just tell me what to do. As a matter of fact, I'm not a bad cook. I've been fixing my own meals since I was a theater student—and that was, I hate to admit it, almost twenty years ago."

"You're a professional actor, then," Pamela inquired as she took the cup from him. "Tell you what—I'll do the measuring, but you do the beating. My arms feel like they're going to drop off."

Rob cheerfully agreed to that arrangement, and as she measured flour, sugar, spices, milk, rum and fresh fruit into the large container, he propped his narrow hips against the opposite counter, folded his arms over his broad chest and watched her.

A shiver ran down Pamela's spine. Though she had her back to him, she could feel his dark eyes studying her slender but curvaceous body. To mask her reaction, she repeated her question. "You're a real actor, not just a part-time one for the festival?"

"Yes, I'm a real actor," he informed her in his resonant baritone, "though performing is a secondary part of my career now. I'm the dramaturge at the Folger."

Startled by this statement, she set down her measuring cup. "Dramaturge? What in the world is that?"

"Essentially," Rob began, and she knew from his tone that he'd answered the question many times, "I'm the literary manager for the classical theater

43

productions. I'm responsible for explaining the text to the actors, and making sure they really understand what's going on in the play from a literary standpoint."

She shifted around and faced him. "You mean the actors don't understand the plays they're performing in?"

Rob shrugged. "Often the references in a seventeenth century script are pretty obscure to twentieth century actors and they need someone to interpret terms and allusions."

"And you're qualified to do that?" she pressed.

He nodded and grinned. "I hope so. I was awake for most of my classes in graduate school."

Now Pamela was all ears. "You have a Master's?"

"Actually, a PhD—my thesis was on Renaissance drama."

"Really? That's fascinating!" So he wasn't the rootless vagabond she'd imagined, Pamela told herself with a distinct feeling of pleasure. "I love the Folger," she volunteered. "I attend all the productions there." As she spoke she thought of the famous Shakespeare research library's reproduction of the seventeenth century Globe Theatre. The theater, with its balconies, wooden railings and small stage, was intimate. Often, as she sat in the audience, she felt as if she were in the middle of the stage action.

"How long have you been at the Folger?" she finally asked.

"Six years," Rob answered casually. "I started out doing a bit of acting there. I've only been their dramaturge for the past two years."

"Do you still perform in any of the plays?"

"Occasionally."

Pamela's expression was rapt. Perhaps she'd seen him perform. "What parts have you played?"

Smiling at her, Rob picked up her spoon to flourish it

like a scepter. "Macbeth and King Lear at your service."

Pamela was delighted. "Oh, I've seen you, then," she exclaimed. "You were terrific as Lear." She paused and stared at his chiseled features, thinking how different the role of the aging king was from the romantic swashbuckler he was impersonating at the festival. It was hard to imagine the same man playing both parts, but he'd done it—and very successfully. He was apparently an accomplished actor.

Amused by her enthusiasm, Rob continued to smile down at her. But then, over her shoulder, he noticed that she'd finished assembling the ingredients for muffin batter. Putting his hands around her waist, he gently but firmly set her aside and took her place in front of the bowl. There, he began beating the heavy mixture vigorously. Momentarily disconcerted by the touch of his hands and the ease with which he'd lifted her, Pamela stood watching him with an almost breathless feeling of excitement.

Her gaze traveled over him, noting the snug fit of his jeans over his narrow masculine buttocks and the way his muscles rippled under his shirt as he worked. But then, suddenly irritated by her out-of-proportion reaction to this man, she dragged her eyes away from him and began moving around the kitchen to straighten up. But as she worked, she was still vividly aware of his vital, masculine presence. And when he began to hum a lively tune in a rich baritone, her head jerked up.

"What are you singing?" she asked curiously.

There was a wicked glint in Rob's eyes. "I'll teach you the words:

> *"Here's to ye absent Lords, may they*
> *Long in foreign country stay*
> *Drinking at other ladies' boards*
> *The health of other absent Lords."*

Pamela blushed, but she laughed too. "A bit risqué, sir," she teased.

"Now it's my turn to be inquisitor," he retorted good-humoredly. "Tell me about Pamela Stewart."

She fumbled for words. "There's really not much to tell."

"Ah ha, the lady of mystery returns."

Pamela had to smile at that. If her life were anything, it certainly wasn't mysterious. Everyday, she got up and went to work, ate meals at the usual times, and lived by all society's conventional rules. Yet part of her had always longed for mystery and romance. This man seemed to have a way of bringing that hidden self out.

"I'm just your average muffin lady," she finally quipped. As she spoke, she took the bowl away from him and poured the mixture into the tins.

"Pamela Stewart," Rob murmured at her back, "nothing about you is average."

Trying to ignore what she knew was only a flattering line, but responding to it despite herself, she self-consciously popped the tins into the oven and set the timer. "Shall we have brunch now?" she inquired over her shoulder.

"Fine. All that hard work has made me hungry." While the muffins baked, Rob looked around for a corkscrew to open the champagne.

"I'm sorry," Pamela apologized. "I lent mine to a neighbor, and she hasn't brought it back yet."

He shrugged. "No problem. As a matter of fact, I brought one with me. It's out in my car. I'll go get it and be back in a jiffy."

When he strode out of the kitchen, Pamela began to slice his fresh strawberries. When everything was ready, she pulled out a tray. While she waited for Rob to return, she took out the last batch of muffins and carried the tray out to the sunny deck overlooking the garden behind the kitchen. Carrying the uncorked wine bottle, he joined her a few minutes later.

"Champagne, strawberries, a beautiful day and a beautiful lady to share it with," he commented with his charming grin as he settled back in one of her wrought-iron chairs. "Sounds like a perfect formula for happiness."

It does, Pamela thought. She looked up at the cloudless blue sky, and then down at the garden with its bright splashes of color. The scent of roses wafted up to her nostrils, and she inhaled deeply.

"A toast," Rob proposed, lifting the long-stemmed glass she'd provided. "A bit more elegant this time," he added, gazing into her golden brown eyes. "I want to drink to Pamela Stewart and to my unraveling her mystery."

Coloring slightly at the warmth of his expression, she wondered if this man ever did anything in an ordinary way. Every move he made and every thing he said seemed to possess a special sparkle. Once again she felt as though he had forcibly lifted her from the mundane. In his exciting presence, even the familiar surroundings of her home and garden took on a special aura. The colors of the geraniums, petunias and white ever-blooming roses seemed sharper. And she'd never really stopped to notice how beautiful the thick foliage on the cherry tree was at this time of year. It was as if being in Rob's company heightened all her senses.

But her awareness of the details of her surroundings was only a backdrop to her supercharged consciousness of the magnetic man sitting across the table. His dark eyes were studying her features as though he truly were trying to unravel some of her secrets. Only there weren't any to discover, she thought a bit sadly.

"So far, I've put together the following clues about

47

you." He raised a tan hand and began ticking points off on long, well-cared-for fingers. "You're either an executive at some fancy firm, or you're independently wealthy." He gestured at the interior of her elegantly furnished townhouse. "Or," he added with a twinkle, "you've got a sugar daddy."

Pamela quickly raised a hand and denied the latter. "You were right on the first count. I'm with the Harley Rutherford Foundation."

He took a contemplative sip of his champagne. "Hmm, they've funded some of our projects at the library."

"I'm a grants administrator," she admitted. "Now, tell me something else about Pamela Stewart," she challenged, getting into the spirit of the game.

"Let's see, on the way in from the car I took a peek at your living room. I can deduce from the way you've furnished your place that you like fine things." He picked up a bright red strawberry and proffered it to her. After she'd accepted the sweet fruit and popped it in her mouth, he went on. "You probably haunt antique stores and craft shops. And I'll bet you like art museums."

"So far, so good," Pamela conceded with a laugh. It was a trifle unnerving to find him so observant. Obviously, while she'd been speculating about him, his thoughts had been running along similar lines.

"Actually, I knew all along that you didn't have a sugar daddy. This is a woman's apartment."

"What makes you say that?"

"On my little self-guided tour, I noticed that there was only one toothbrush in your bathroom. And I was pleased to note the absence of a man's bathrobe on the hook. But it's more than that," he went on as her jaw dropped.

"There's no copy of *Playboy* or *Esquire* in your stack of magazines. . . ."

"You snoop!" Pamela protested, throwing a strawberry at him.

He caught it neatly, put it in his mouth and chewed with obvious enjoyment. "True. I have no shame."

Pamela burst into laughter, and it was on that lighthearted note that they finished the champagne, fruit and delicious warm muffins.

When the food was gone, Rob leaned back and patted his flat stomach appreciatively. "Now that we've started the day out so well, what shall we do next?"

Pamela gave him an inquiring look. "Don't you have to go to work?"

"No, my schedule is flexible today. What about you?"

"It's my vacation," she acknowledged.

Rob's smile widened. "Then, if it's a vacation, let's make it a proper one. How about a trip to the zoo?"

"The zoo?" Pamela stared at him for a moment. She hadn't been to the zoo in ages. But suddenly, she realized, caught up in his enthusiasm, that was exactly what she wanted to do.

Rising to his feet, he took her hand and looked critically down at her flour-streaked face and denims. "I think you look charming with spotted jeans and wispy braids, but the monkeys tend to be very particular about their visitors. I'll straighten up down here while you change."

A few minutes later, Pamela was searching through her closet. She finally selected a pale yellow sundress. After she'd brushed out her hair and applied makeup, she glanced critically at her image and then rejoined Rob downstairs. True to his word, he'd tidied the kitchen, and it was now spotless.

"Much better," he complimented, running an appreciative eye over her outfit. Then, taking her hand again, he led her out the door to a vintage Volvo sports car parked out in front, and they were on their way.

It was an August day that seemed to belong in September, and the cooler weather, after weeks of intense heat, had brought other visitors and strollers to the National Zoo.

"I guess we're not the only ones playing hooky," Rob remarked as he pointed to other women and men in business attire wandering around the pathways and munching on peanuts. After buying a bag for Pamela, he led her to the monkey house, where they admired the acrobatic antics of the animals. To Pamela's astonished amusement, Rob did very accurate imitations of some of the creatures. And when she pointed out a somber-looking baboon, Rob insisted on trying to "cheer him up."

"Come on, old fellow, it can't be as bad as that," he argued.

The ape stared back mournfully.

Thrusting out his lower lip and hunching his shoulders, Rob mimicked the creature's posture, sending the people around them into gales of laughter. But his subject remained stone-faced.

"Reminds me of an audience I played to a few years back," the actor remarked with a grimace.

During the next hour Rob and Pamela admired the sleek tigers and lions, hissed at the snakes, and held a one-way conversation with a fat white polar bear. But the highlight of their afternoon turned out to be their visit to the pandas.

A gift of the People's Republic of China, Ling-Ling and Hsing-Hsing had been endearing themselves to visitors of the zoo for twelve years. But though Pamela had read accounts of their troubled courtship, she'd never seen the furry black and white creatures before.

"Oh, they're adorable," she exclaimed, "like oversize teddy bears!"

As she and Rob paused in front of the windows, the two pandas were in separate enclosures.

"That's Ling-Ling on the far right," Rob informed her.

"How can you tell? They look the same to me."

He pointed at the dish of sweet potatoes mixed in with the apples, bamboo, carrots and rice that the female bear was nibbling. "They're trying to fatten her up, so she's the only one who gets the sweet potatoes."

Pamela cocked her head at the 250-pound creature. "She looks pretty hefty to me now."

"But apparently not to Hsing-Hsing. The zoo officials have been encouraging them to mate for years, but so far not with much success."

"How do you happen to know so much about these pandas?"

"I read an article about it in the *Post* recently."

Pamela glanced over at the male panda, who was leaning comfortably back on a rock and contentedly munching on his own afternoon snack. "Well, I've read that Hsing-Hsing is the one at fault. He's not much of a lover."

Rob chuckled and shot her an amused look. "Yes, poor fellow. Apparently, his technique is lacking. But you have to feel sorry for the unfortunate, beleaguered male, with all those eyes following his every move. All those charts, graphs, cameras and curious stares would intimidate a Don Juan extraordinaire."

He was referring to the "panda watch," Pamela knew. She'd read an account of it recently. During mating season each spring, volunteers for the zoo kept a hopeful vigil on the animals' amatory behavior. Any reports of a coupling were greeted with media coverage from newspapers and television and radio stations and great jubilation from zoo officials.

"I agree," Pamela said. "But you have to feel sorry

for Ling-Ling, too. Just look at the way he's ignoring her. He's like a middle-aged man who plops himself in front of the television each night and doesn't even know his poor wife exists."

"I don't think it's that," Rob demurred, a roguish glint in his dark eyes. "He's just shy and inexperienced. What he needs is a few lessons in the proper way to treat a lady."

Pamela cast him a mischievous glance from under her lashes. "Oh, and could you give him some?"

"I don't speak panda, but if I did, there are a few pointers I might be able to pass along."

This was getting interesting, Pamela thought. "Like what?"

He grinned, flashing teeth that were very white in the bronze of his face. "Are you really interested in finding out? Because, if so, I'll be glad to oblige—in some more private spot, of course," he added, gesturing at the crowd around the panda house.

Pamela felt heat rise to her cheeks and averted her eyes. "I stepped right into that, didn't I?"

Smiling, Rob took her hand and squeezed it. "Yes, you did, but I found it charming. Just like everything about you." He glanced at his watch. "It's almost two o'clock. I have to give a class at three this afternoon. Why don't we get ice cream cones, and then I'll take you home."

A half an hour later, as Rob rounded the corner in his Volvo, Pamela regretted seeing her townhouse come into view. She'd enjoyed their afternoon together so much that she hated to have their outing end.

But when her escort pulled up in front of her building, instead of getting out to open the door on the passenger side, he turned her way and took her hand lightly in his. "Pamela, I've had such a good time with you today! How about spending tomorrow with me—if you have nothing better to do, that is."

A tingle of excitement ran through Pamela's body. What in the world could she have better to do than be with Rob Darcy? she asked herself. She was beginning to feel like a lonely child with a wonderful new playmate. Aloud, however, she queried, "Can you get away from work again?"

"I think it can be arranged. But we'll have to leave early if we're going to get to the beach before the roads crowd up."

"The beach?"

He gave her a questioning look. "Can you be ready with a bathing suit and towel by seven in the morning?"

"Sure," she agreed. "I'll be waiting out in front with a picnic basket." It seemed only fair to make lunch, since he'd provided such a delicious outdoor feast on their first meeting.

In an affectionate gesture, he tugged at a lock of her hair. "Sounds like we'll have the ingredients for another perfect day!"

Rob's prediction turned out to be accurate. When they arrived at Ocean City on Maryland's Eastern Shore the next morning, the sky was a halcyon blue, the sun was a promising blaze of gold and the white sand stretching along the ocean front looked soft and inviting. Though they found a spot near the water easily, the beach was far from deserted. Seminude bathing beauties in string bikinis were already stretched out here and there on the sand soaking up the rays. And nearby, a small boy and girl with sand pails were industriously building an elaborate castle.

Rob gestured at the children and smiled indulgently. "Reminds me of my youth. I have a weakness for public beaches like this."

"Oh? Why is that?" Pamela asked. As she spoke she wriggled out of her cutoffs and then unbuttoned her shirt. Beneath it, she wore a simple white one piece suit.

It hadn't occurred to her that she'd feel self-conscious about appearing before Rob in her modest bathing costume. But when she shed the blouse and glanced up to find his dark gaze taking in the lines of her figure with intense interest, she felt almost naked beneath his scrutiny and wished for the concealing folds of the long skirt she'd be wearing each weekend at the festival. To ease her sudden fit of embarrassment, she asked her question in a different way. "Did you spend a lot of time at the seashore when you were a youngster?"

He nodded and began to unzip his own jeans. As he stripped them from his legs, she remembered how his muscular thighs had looked in the stretchy material of his tights. But Rob's next words banished the image of him in Renaissance costume. "My mother deserted my father when I was small," he said, looking off at the ocean. "As a single parent, he had a hard time coping with me when I wasn't in school. So summers I was shipped off to an aunt who had a cottage in Cape May."

Pamela was startled by this information. "I'm sorry about your mother, Rob. Did you have an unhappy childhood?"

He laughed at her and then reached down and pulled her to her feet. "Let's take a walk along the beach while it's still fairly empty." Taking her hand firmly in his, he led her to the water's edge where they began to stroll on the hard-packed sand. "To answer your question," he continued, "no, I didn't have an unhappy childhood. I hardly remembered my mother, and I seem to have a pretty resilient nature. I just wasn't made for unhappiness, and so I make the best of situations."

Thoughtfully, Pamela glanced down at her toes and watched a small wave wash around her ankles. What Rob had said about himself seemed true, she thought. With his self-confident, sunny disposition, he was the sort of person who wouldn't let life's knocks and disappointments get him down.

"How about you?" he was asking. "What kind of childhood did you have?"

"My father died when I was seven. My mother raised me by herself. But, really, my childhood was very ordinary in most ways."

Rob looked down at the top of her head quizzically, thinking how pretty she looked with her lightly tanned skin glowing and her rich hair falling in waves around her shoulders. "That's hard to believe," he commented. "I've already said it, but I'll say it again. There's nothing ordinary about you. I wish I'd known you as a teenager. You must have been a beauty."

She laughed and shook her head at that notion. "On the contrary, I was an ugly duckling. I was skinny, wore braces and was painfully shy."

Rob stopped walking and turned Pamela toward him so that she was very conscious of the breadth of his naked tanned shoulders and his lean hips encased in brief, dark blue trunks. "If you were an ugly duckling then, you're a beautiful swan now. But something tells me you don't realize it." He put his hands on her shoulders and kneaded them gently.

Pamela laughed self-consciously. "I really wasn't much to look at. I didn't date at all in high school."

"Not at all?"

She shook her head. "I guess my time was pretty full, what with working at a local store, studying and going to school. But," she added, lifting her shoulders, "I really wasn't popular with the boys. And they're still not beating down my door."

Rob shook his head, then leaned down and gently kissed her forehead. "Pamela, why are you so down on yourself? What am I going to do with you?"

His face was so close to hers that she could see the texture of his skin and the laugh lines around his handsome dark eyes. Her breasts tingled at his nearness, and she took a step backward to give herself a bit of breathing space. "Well," she suggested, her expression lightening, "you could take a swim with me and then eat the lunch I packed. How does that sound?"

"Great!" he answered, once more closing the distance between them. As though she weighed no more than a feather, he picked her up in his arms and strode into the ocean while she giggled and protested ineffectually.

The rest of the morning seemed to drift by in a pleasant golden haze. After their swim, they sunbathed, talked and admired their surroundings. Then they ate their picnic lunch and took a stroll on Ocean City's boardwalk. Rob stopped at one of the arcades that lined the wooden thoroughfare and played a lively game of "Red Baron" with her. As she enthusiastically vied with him to shoot down airplanes, Pamela laughed like a carefree teenager. Later, Rob insisted on buying her an Ocean City tee-shirt as a souvenir.

"Oh, Rob, I've had a wonderful time these past two days," she confided as he led her back to his car.

"Me too," he agreed, settling her into the passenger seat and then walking around to get in. "But I'm not ready for it to end. I have to check in at the Folger this afternoon. How about coming with me? Then, afterward, I'd like you to have dinner with me."

While he backed out of his parking space and pulled onto the main road, Pamela watched his strong, capable hands on the wheel. The sports car's sun roof was open, and the summer breeze whipped a lock of black hair over his forehead, giving him a piratical look. It reminded Pamela of their first picnic, when his kiss had evoked such a fiery response in her. Since that time his kisses had been only lightly affectionate. Nevertheless, though their hours together had been in daylight, talking and getting to know each other, the sexual attraction that had brought them together in the first place was always just below the seemingly casual surface. Surely, Pamela told herself, if she agreed to spend the evening with Rob, he would kiss her as he had earlier. And where might that lead?

Leaning against the headrest and closing her eyes, she let the pleasant summer breeze play over her flushed skin. She didn't know what would happen if Rob Darcy kissed her properly. And right now she refused to worry about it. "Yes," she said aloud. "I'd love to have dinner with you."

4

Much later that afternoon, after a quick stop at Pamela's townhouse so she could change clothes, they drove off down the streets of Washington, past the Capitol building and Library of Congress. Nimbly, the red Volvo darted through the side streets behind the library as Rob looked for a place to park. Finally, he found a spot on a shady avenue lined with renovated townhouses. After helping Pamela out of the car, he led her to the impressive white marble structure that housed the famous Folger theater and library.

With Rob at her side, she walked up the marble steps leading to a set of glass doors decorated with what looked like wrought-iron scrollwork. As always, she was both excited and impressed by what the building stood for as well as by what it contained—the most complete collection of original Shakespearean material in the world.

Once inside the entry, Pamela peeked at the gift shop

on the right. It boasted posters depicting Queen Elizabeth and the Globe Theatre, as well as an assortment of books, scarves, jewelry and postcards. To her left she could glimpse the Great Hall with its high ceilings, Tudor-style paneling, flag stone floors and display cases. Beyond that, she knew, lay the theater.

Rob waved as he led her past the guard and into the corridor where the private offices were located. His was at the end of the hall. When he ushered her in, she gave a pleased exclamation.

"I'll trade offices with you," she offered, privately contrasting the warm atmosphere of his quarters with her own company's rather sterile environment. On the office floor was a slightly rumpled Heriz in brilliant shades of red and blue. As she admired the beautiful oriental rug, she sank into the worn red velvet seat of one of the carved chairs in front of Rob's oak desk. Lifting her eyes, she found herself face to face with a huge photograph of John Barrymore playing Hamlet. Two other of Rob's office walls were decorated with several old-fashioned paintings depicting scenes from various Shakespearean productions.

"I'm glad you like it," Rob responded. "I'm afraid I'm a bit spoiled," he added, looking at the massive oak bookcases lining the wall opposite his desk. They were stuffed with books on Shakespeare and the Renaissance period.

"Excuse me a moment," he added, "I have to check in with my secretary." When he returned, he was smiling. "I've looked at my messages, and there's nothing that can't wait till tomorrow. Let me give you the abbreviated grand tour." Taking her hand, he led her back out into the hall.

"I've heard the Folger has a ghost or two?" Pamela remarked as her heels clicked on the flagstone floor.

"More than one, if you believe the reports. One is

supposed to be a nineteenth century actor in full stage regalia. But my favorite is in here," he remarked as they approached a plaster arch.

Taking her arm, Rob walked her into a large conference room with an oak table and two display cases holding Shakespearean memorabilia, including a bracelet woven from the hair of actor Edwin Booth.

"The Victorians went in for that kind of thing," he explained as they strolled past. "Do you see my ghost?"

Pamela looked around. All she could see was a large oil painting dominating the conference table. It depicted the famous scene in which Hamlet reproaches his mother while Polonius lies dead behind the arras.

Rob grinned at her confusion. "Here, follow me," he said, stepping to the other end of the table and walking to the right side of the painting. From that angle, Pamela discovered, she actually could make out the faint outlines of the ghost of Hamlet's father.

When she made the discovery, she smiled into Rob's lustrous dark eyes. "That's wonderful. He just seems to materialize."

"Yes, doesn't he though. I'd seen this painting dozens of times, but I didn't even know he was there until I was sitting at this table during a meeting and I looked up. There he was!" Rob shook his head. "But I have something else interesting to show you."

Next he led her through the medieval reading room with its balustrades, galleries and stained-glass window depicting the "Seven Ages of Man."

As she examined the inscription over the spot where Mr. and Mrs. Folger's ashes were encased, Pamela read under her breath, "Dedicated to the glory of Shakespeare and to the greater glory of God."

Taking her arm, Rob whispered in her ear, "Some people say they had their priorities reversed, but you'd never know it around here. Now let me show you the 'Holy of Holies.' "

After he had ushered her through a series of rooms, Pamela suddenly found herself in an oak-paneled chamber confronting what looked like a bank vault door.

Rob tapped it significantly. "This is where we keep the treasure. And I'm one of the honored few," he added dramatically, "who can pass through this door." Taking a set of keys out of his pocket, he opened the vault and led her into an elevator.

"Where are we going?" Pamela demanded.

"To see the crown jewels—the place where we keep the books published before 1640, including the seventy-nine copies of the 1623 first folio edition of *Mr. William Shakespeare's comedies, histories and tragedies.*

When the elevator came to a stop, he guided her to an underground atmosphere-controlled room filled with leather-bound volumes.

"The original of Chaucer's *Canterbury Tales*," Rob said, taking a handsome tome from a shelf and opening it. "Published in 1478."

Pamela gasped. "But it looks like it's in almost perfect condition."

"It is. Only a few pages have been repaired. And how about this?" he went on, replacing the Chaucer and hefting a huge green box from a lower shelf. Carrying it as though he were a ten-year-old with a much-prized birthday present, he placed it on a small table and ceremoniously opened it. Inside, was a huge, red velvet-bound bible with silver clasps.

"Oh, it's beautiful!"

"It belonged to Queen Elizabeth I. She read from it every day." Rob's long fingers touched the velvet almost reverently, and Pamela couldn't help smiling.

61

She never would have guessed the dashing swordsman of the festival was a bibliophile. But it was obvious that he loved these rare old books and was deriving a great deal of pleasure from showing them off to her.

Moving quickly through that room and the next, he opened precious volume after volume, pointing out Henry VIII's inscription—"This Book is Mine," scrawled boldly across the bottom of a page of Cicero, the signature of Francis Bacon, and—the crowning gem—Shakespeare's first folio.

Handing her the huge dark leather tome, he said with a smile, "You're holding something worth a million dollars."

But when Pamela tried to hand it back, he insisted that she open the prized volume and examine the brown-edged pages.

It was a full hour before they returned to the upper floor where Rob's office was located, and by that time Pamela knew more about Shakespeare, the Renaissance period, and the Folger than she'd ever learned in her college English classes.

"Hungry?" Rob asked as they strolled back into his comfortable office.

As if in answer to his question, her stomach rumbled hollowly, and she instinctively put a hand over it.

"Guess so," Rob commented with a chuckle. "Well, I hope you like Spanish food, because I've made dinner reservations at El Bodegon."

Pamela glanced down at the simple blue cotton dress she'd changed into after returning from the beach. "Do you think this will do?"

Rob's gaze touched her warmly. "With you in it, it'll do beautifully."

She smiled. "It sounds like a wonderful idea, then."

At that moment, a familiar voice interrupted their conversation. "Rob, I have a question . . ."

Turning, Pamela recognized a small, dapper figure in

a gray sports jacket and slacks. Her face lit up. "Jake—Jake the Jester! What are you doing here?"

The little man glanced from her to Rob and then grinned. "I was about to ask the same of you."

"I've been showing the lady all our wonders," Rob explained.

"Then how did you miss me?" Jake demanded impishly. "Or were you saving the best for last?"

"You see, he really is a jester," Rob joked, turning back to Pamela. "Only we don't let him wear his costume while he edits *The Shakespeare Quarterly* for us."

Jake merely laughed, and soon he and Pamela were talking easily about the festival and their plans for the following weekend. Rob watched them, beginning to wonder how well they knew one another. Though he wasn't usually the jealous type, their camaraderie made him uneasy. He couldn't help feeling that Pamela was his own special discovery. Jake could be charming when he wanted. Finding that he was on such good terms with her was irrationally disturbing.

Glancing at his watch, Rob interrupted their conversation. "Since the two of you are already friends, why don't I leave you here, Pamela, while I go across the street to my house and change into something a bit more presentable than jeans."

Despite his light tone, Pamela thought she detected a slight note of impatience. But when he returned twenty minutes later, dressed in an elegantly cut light gray suit that emphasized his dark good looks, he was as charming as ever.

"I'm going to reclaim this lovely lady," he told his colleague. Politely but firmly, he took her arm. "I intend to feed her some good Spanish food."

"As long as its just food and not any of your lines," Jake retorted with a mock scowl.

Rob began to lead Pamela away. "When I compliment this lady," he tossed back over his shoulder, "I'm not feeding her a line. I'm telling her the truth."

El Bodegón, the restaurant where Rob had reserved a table, was one of the few Spanish eating places in the nation's capital. Located just a short distance from Dupont Circle, the white-painted brick building with its red awning was a renovated townhouse.

"Our reservations were for seven o'clock," he remarked as he parked the car and helped Pamela out of the low-slung automobile. "So, we're right on the dot. That should give us time to eat before the flamenco dancer comes on."

"Flamenco dancer," she repeated. "They have a floor show here?"

Rob winked. "Oh, definitely—a flamenco guitarist too. Eating dinner at El Bodegón is an experience."

Once inside the white-washed, half-timbered interior, they were shown to a candlelit table downstairs close to a tiny stage. Rob ordered a pitcher of sangria, and while they sipped the chilled red wine brimming with small pieces of apple, orange and lemon, they studied the menu.

"Why don't we start with tapas?" Rob suggested.

"What are those?"

"A type of Spanish hors d'oeuvre served in taverns. You've got your choice of pulpo, jabon, serrano, chorizos or calamares."

"I'll try the pulpo," she said, liking the sound of the unknown word and feeling adventurous. "By the way," she asked after giving her order, "what is it?"

Rob's face was perfectly bland. "You've ordered marinated baby octopus."

Pamela blinked. "Oh."

Despite her initial reaction, however, the pulpo turned out to be tender and tasty. And the zarzuela which followed, a combination of fresh mussels, shrimp, squid, crab and fish simmered in herbs and brandy, was heavenly. As Pamela ate, Rob made sure her sangria glass was full, and by the time she finished her dinner she was feeling mellow.

"You told me yesterday that before you went back to school, you were a full-time actor?" Pamela inquired.

Rob nodded. "Yes, right after college I struck out on my own."

"That sounds scary to me."

His dark eyebrows lifted. "Scary?"

"Well, isn't there a lot of uncertainty living from hand to mouth, from one play to the next—never knowing how long a play will run, or where the next part will come from?"

Rob shrugged. "Oh, yes, but that's part of the life. It's a challenge. You're constantly testing yourself against other actors—no chance of stagnating." He chuckled. "But there *were* lean times. Twice I was forced to hock my watch in order to eat. And once I had to hide my car so it wouldn't get repossessed. I'd shift it from one block to the other, dodging the repossession goons," he recalled, chuckling at the memory. "At the time I was terrified because my next part depended on my having transportation. Finally, I got things straightened out though."

Pamela stared at him in amazement. "I can't even imagine living like that!" she exclaimed. Her life had always been so carefully planned. She'd always had money tucked away in a savings account and been armed against the vagaries of fate with insurance policies and money market investments. Having to pawn a piece of jewelry or worry about paying for groceries seemed to her like stepping into the twilight zone.

"You get used to it," Rob was saying. "Even my job now, secure as it looks, is dependent on a grant. I have to get down on my knees and pray for a renewal each spring. So far I've been lucky; my supplications the last couple of years have been answered." He gave her a roguish wink. "Must be my clean living."

"Must be." Pamela laughed and raised her glass. "To more clean living and more grants." But inwardly she was marveling all over again at how different they were. No one knew better than she how chancy grants were. Yet, despite Rob's words, he didn't look in the least threatened by the uncertainty of his lifestyle. He was not the type of man to huddle in a safe corner. He would always go out and challenge fate, taming it to his will. She certainly couldn't imagine living with someone like that. But experiencing his exhilarating company for this brief interlude was very exciting.

The waiter was just taking their empty plates away when the flamenco dancer, clad in a yellow dress with a full, ruffled skirt and a matching flower in her jet black hair took the stage. For the next fifteen minutes she swirled and tapped her heels to the colorful Andalusian music of the guitarist. The dramatic melodies, rhythmic stomping and clapping of the exotic-looking dancer and the passionate singing of her accompanist stirred Pamela's blood.

And when the performance was over, she looked across the table at Rob.

"Stirs the passion in my soul," he murmured. "How about you?"

"It does make my blood a bit warmer," she agreed. And, in truth, she felt alive with excitement. As she studied the man across from her, she thought he stood out against the dark background of the dimly lit restaurant. His tan skin looked so vibrant and healthy that she wanted to stroke his cheek. She smiled at him with radiant eyes. Feeling a bit bold, she reached across the table and took his strong, dark hand in hers.

"I don't remember when I've had such a lovely time."

He smiled back at her. "Me too. But it's still not over.

You haven't even tried drinking from the porrón yet," he said, pointing at a middle-aged man at the next table. Shouts of laughter rang from the group as the man tilted his head back, opened his mouth and drank a stream of golden wine from the spout of a teakettle-shaped glass flagon.

"That's the porrón," Rob explained. "It's a Spanish tavern tradition to see how much you can drink from it without drenching your clothes."

"Who's the man pouring it?" she asked, noticing the curly-haired young man standing next to the open-mouthed customer.

"That's José; he's quite an expert and never spills on any of his customers. Here, I'll show you," he added, motioning José to their table.

"Oh, no," Pamela began to protest, fearing that she would make a fool of herself. "José may be skilled, but I'd probably get it all over me."

Despite her objections, in the next moment the smiling wielder of the porrón was at her side persuading her to give it a try.

"Just tip your head back, señorita, and open your mouth. That's all you need to do," he promised. Feeling her cheeks turn pink, Pamela's gaze darted around the room as though she were searching out a place to hide. Everyone in the restaurant was looking at her, she noted with alarm. And Rob was sitting back watching the scene with an amused smile. There was no way she was going to get out of this, she realized. Finally, she did as José asked, opening her mouth and tilting her head back. He tipped his flagon and a stream of wine arched through the air to land neatly on her tongue and slide down her throat. Marveling that it worked so well, she began to feel her mouth filling up.

Starting to laugh, Pamela raised her hand for him to stop.

"Brava!" exclaimed Rob and Jose while the friendly people at the next table cheered and clapped.

Laughing and blushing, Pamela took a bow and then insisted that Rob try a turn with the porrón. He acquiesced, swallowing the stream of golden wine with aplomb before José finally left their table for another.

"I'm jealous. You do everything well," she remarked lightly.

Rob grinned wickedly. "Wait till you get to know me better." He paused while she absorbed that and then added, "Actually I'm plagued by flaws. But I'm doing my best to keep the chinks in my armor hidden from you."

Pamela shook her head. He was certainly doing a good job. So far the man seemed about perfect.

"Ready to go?" Rob asked after paying the check.

"Not really," Pamela admitted, "but I guess it is getting late." Even as she said the polite words, she couldn't hold back a pang of disappointment.

As they stepped out of the restaurant into the cool evening Pamela's legs felt a bit wobbly. She wasn't sure whether it was from the liberal portions of Spanish wine she'd imbibed or the heady feelings that spending the day with Rob had generated. Maybe it was both, she told herself with an inward smile as he helped her into the front seat of his car. Having Rob for a companion was intoxicating all by itself.

And if just spending the day with him was so wonderful, what would it be like to stay the night with him? Glancing at his chiseled profile, she noted the way his thick curly hair brushed his white shirt collar and admired the firm thrust of his chin and the straight line of his nose. Just then, he turned and caught her staring at him. His ebony eyes brightened, and he reached across, caught her hand and raised it to his lips.

"Lesson number one for Hsing-Hsing on how to treat a lady?" Pamela teased with a soft laugh.

He answered her laugh with one of his own. But when they pulled to a stoplight seconds later, he leaned over, took her in his arms and kissed her soundly. "Lesson number two," he murmured into her cascading hair.

They both laughed then. But when he'd returned to the wheel and once more was piloting them through Washington, she reached over and touched his shoulder lightly. He'd started a current of electricity flowing between them, and she couldn't bring herself to break the circuit. Just that brief contact with Rob was enough to make the surface of her skin alive with tingling sensations.

"We're not going toward my apartment," she said, noticing that they were once more headed in the direction of the Folger.

"No. It's early yet, and I thought we could go back to my place for a nightcap."

Pamela felt a little twinge of apprehension. She had no doubt that if she objected, Rob would take her back home. But the truth was that she didn't want to say good-bye to him yet. Their time together had been such a release from her straitjacket office world. At the zoo yesterday, then today at the beach and later at El Bodegón, she had been looking at the world around her with the wide-eyed wonder of a child. She owed that fresh perception to Rob, and even though she'd be seeing him at the festival in a couple of days, she simply wasn't ready to part from him.

Leaning back against the headrest of his sleek car, she acquiesced.

Rob's home turned out to be a turn-of-the-century white-washed brick townhouse.

"Oh, it's charming," Pamela exclaimed as they walked together up the stone path that led through the small, ivy-covered front yard.

"One of the benefits of my job." Rob unlocked the

front door and ushered her into a center hall. It boasted polished wide board floors and high ceilings. Through the archway she glimpsed a formal dining room furnished with a Hepplewhite sideboard and a large mahogany Chippendale table and chairs.

The living room turned out to be even more impressive. Fine oriental rugs covered the handsome wood floor. A formal Williamsburg wallpaper in blue and white was accented by crown molding in the darker hue.

Sinking into a damask-covered loveseat, she ran a hand over the rich material. "I'm impressed by your taste."

"Don't be," he remarked, leaning easily against the mantel and looking down at her. "The furniture comes with the place. People often leave bequests of fine antiques to the Folger, and they wind up in our offices and the houses rented to employees. Though," he added, "I've grown very fond of all this." He gestured around the elegantly appointed room.

"I should think so," Pamela remarked, watching him stride across the floor to the Sheridan cabinet. He opened it to reveal an array of crystal decanters.

"What can I offer you? There's sherry, brandy and several liqueurs," he said, ticking off the names.

"I'll go with the sherry."

"The right choice for the end of a Spanish meal," he remarked lightly as he filled two small stemmed glasses. Handing her a glass, he said conversationally, "There's an interesting story about the way they age this. Years ago, it was carried as ballast on ships that sailed to Australia." He grinned. "The idea was that the rocking motion in the casks aged it perfectly. My experts tell me, however, that when diesels were substituted for sailing ships, the quality of the sherry deteriorated."

Sitting down next to her on the small loveseat, he put his arm along the back and caught a strand of her hair over his finger. "I like the silky feel of your hair. And I like the way you wear it, loose and free."

At his words, Pamela felt a bit like an impostor. Although she'd worn her hair down for the festival, normally, she pinned it in a twist. She also dressed much more conservatively than Rob had yet seen her. But she was very glad that she'd elected to brush her hair and leave it down for today. Looking over at Rob, she mused that sitting there in his dimly lit living room, sipping the rich fire of the sherry, she felt like a different woman—one who, with few qualms, could enjoy being close to an exciting man. And they *were* very close. As Pamela gazed up into his deeply attractive countenance she noticed how velvety his dark eyes now appeared.

Taking her glass from her fingers and placing it on the tea table, he pulled her against him and slowly lowered his mouth to hers. As she felt his firm lips she realized that she'd been waiting for this contact between them all day. The kiss took her back to that moment when they'd come so near to making love on the grass the weekend before. All the aches and longings she'd repressed then seemed to flame up as though life-giving oxygen had been blown into a banked fire. Wrapping her arms around his wide shoulders, she stroked the strong line of his back.

She felt his mouth nibble gently at the outer curve of her ear. "Ummm," he murmured. "You smell like jasmine."

Pressing her body closer to him so that her breasts rubbed against the light wool of his suit jacket, she allowed her hands to explore the back of his neck where his hair brushed his collar. She loved the feel of the thick strands. As she curled one around her finger, she was surprised by the silky texture.

Rob moved his mouth to her jaw and dropped a line of kisses there. Arching her neck, Pamela closed her eyes and enjoyed the delicious sensations his caresses provoked. Her hands were still at the back of his head, stroking his hair.

"Oh, Rob . . ." she moaned, as his lips traveled down the column of her throat and found the sensitive hollow.

"You taste good, Pamela Stewart," he whispered. "I'm glad I turned down the flan at El Bodegón. I'd rather have you for dessert." Lifting his head, he grinned at her wickedly, and she couldn't repress her laughter.

"But you said you didn't have room for dessert," she pointed out.

"Changed my mind." He pulled her to him again and molded his lips to hers. This kiss was more demanding, and Pamela found herself yielding to its insistence without a struggle. His tongue found its way beyond her teeth to meet with hers. Pamela could taste the brandy in his mouth. It mingled with the sherry she had sipped, creating a heady mixture. The effect was so intoxicating that she hardly noticed when he slipped her jacket off one shoulder and pushed the spaghetti strap aside.

When his mouth finally lifted, he said, "It's getting awfully warm in here." After shrugging off his own jacket, he gently removed hers as well. Pamela didn't even consider protesting. At that moment, she wanted this man as much as he seemed to want her.

Taking her in his arms again, Rob looked ruefully at the small loveseat. "Right now I wish this were a big, cushiony sofa. But we'll just have to make do," he added, lowering her to the damask seat.

"I have the feeling that you make do very well," she whispered, her hands going to the buttons on his shirt. Somewhere in the back of her mind, the staid, conservative Pamela was asking what in the world she was doing. But the Pamela who'd been swept off her feet by Robyn O'Dare ignored that nagging little voice. When the first three buttons of his shirt were open, her fingers slipped inside the fine cotton material to feel the warm flesh beneath. It was sprinkled with crisp hair that teased the sensitive pads of her fingers.

Rob groaned with pleasure. "It feels good to have you touching me," he murmured in her ear. "Don't stop." As he spoke, his hands slid up her rib cage to the soft swell of her breasts beneath the bodice of her sundress. Cupping their fullness in his large hands, he circled her nipples gently with his thumbs. Under the thin fabric, the tips of her breasts were hard with desire.

The feelings he was arousing in Pamela were so delicious that she wanted him *not* to stop. To encourage his intimate caresses, she slid open two more buttons on his shirt and then began to tug it from his waistband.

Delighted by her move, Rob leaned back, finished unbuttoning his shirt and took it off altogether. When it lay discarded on the floor, he put his arms around her waist and kissed her firmly while she ran her palms over the tight muscles of his broad back.

"That feels wonderful," he said huskily. "But it would be even better if I could feel you too." His hands went to the zipper on her dress, and she arched her back as she felt him slide it down. Right now their desires matched perfectly. She wanted, more than anything, to feel her bare skin next to his.

When the dress slipped down around her waist and her swollen breasts were bare, he bent his head to caress them. Taking a nipple in his mouth, he ran an exploring tongue over its crest until Pamela moaned with gathering excitement. As he continued to tease her throbbing breasts, Pamela felt an ache along the inside of her thighs that seemed to gather in a tight knot deep within her.

Again, Rob lifted his dark head and stared unhappily at the small loveseat. Then he looked directly into

Pamela's simmering golden brown eyes. "My lady, either we quit, we land on the floor or we move to my bedroom. What's your pleasure?"

He had phrased his query lightly, but Pamela knew his intent was serious. He was asking her clearly and unequivocally for a decision. But she was unable to think clearly. She wanted him too much to deny him or herself now. "I guess the bed would be preferable to the floor," she murmured throatily.

"Wise decision. The floor could be hard on my knees," Rob joked. But even as he made her laugh, he was pulling her to her feet. When she was standing next to him, he embraced her tightly, dropped a kiss on her breasts and then led her into the next room.

The bedroom was furnished in the same antique style as the living room, but Pamela had only a dim impression of muted colors and elegance as Rob swept her to a large fourposter. In a moment, her dress was sliding from her body to the floor, and she found herself being lifted to the white tufted spread. Rob undid the slim straps of her sandals, stroked her ankles and then set her shoes down on the floor also. Scrutinizing her body hungrily through the shadowy light, he quickly unbuckled his belt and removed the rest of his clothing.

He was truly a beautiful man, she thought, gazing at his naked body. Seeing how magnificently aroused he was, she felt an answering craving in her own femininity and held her arms out to him in a gesture of welcome.

"You're lovely, Pamela," he told her as he lay down next to her. "I've been thinking of having you like this from the first time I saw you. And when I fell at your feet at the festival that day, I was determined we'd be together as we are now." The moonlight filtering in through the open window silvered his profile, and the shadows from a tree outside lent his features a romantic mystery.

She had no idea how she would feel in the morning

about making love to this man. But she refused to consider that now. All she could think about was the moment, and her desire to unite herself with him.

Slowly, with sensual deliberation, Rob began to stroke the hollows and planes of her slim, curved body. Lightly, his sensitive hands touched her forehead, then her cheek. He ran a finger along the line of her lips and then down her throat where he dropped a soft kiss.

It was as though they were memorizing each other's features; while he explored her, she touched him as well. Her fingers fluttered over his high forehead, and she brushed a thumb across the dark sweep of one of his brows. Then she ran a finger down the straight bridge of his nose, and touched his firm lips. "Hmm," she murmured, tugging gently on his mustache. "This is for real, not a prop."

"Oh, the mustache is mine all right," he murmured huskily, "and everything else you see, too." He gave her a mock leer before dipping his head to brush the tips of her breasts with his lips.

Pamela moaned with pleasure. She felt like a dreamer awakening to find her fantasy was real. At first she had floated pleasantly in the gentle warmth of his caresses. But as his hands and mouth became more insistent, exploring her with greater intimacy, her response grew more urgent. His hands slipped down the silky insides of her thighs and she wriggled beneath him with excitement.

"Touch me too, Pamela," he whispered as he kissed the smooth skin of her stomach. "Let me feel your hands on me."

She complied instantly, running her hands along his broad shoulders, wide furred chest and then down to the flat plain of his belly as he slid up next to her. Then her hands went lower, eliciting a moan of pleasure from Rob. When he rolled over on top of her, she could feel the bold thrust of his masculinity pressed against her stomach. Having such tangible proof of how she was affecting him, wrung an even deeper response from her. An ache of desire spread through her.

"You're driving me crazy," Rob growled in her ear. "I want you so much, Pamela."

"I want you too," she whispered back urgently.

Rob's response was instantaneous. In the next moment he was parting her willing thighs and entering her eager warmth.

Pamela's hands cupped his lean buttocks and she could feel the electric desire coursing through him. But though she could sense that his need was urgent, his thrusts were slow and controlled. The realization that he was putting her pleasure ahead of his was like an aphrodisiac to Pamela, and she moved beneath him with fevered motions.

"Oh, Pamela, I knew it would be like this between us," he gasped as his thrusts became deeper and more compelling.

Somewhere inside her, she had known it too, she realized. She felt caught up in a landslide of passion that was sweeping over her. But instead of trying to fight clear, Pamela gloried in the fantastic new sensations that were claiming her.

She felt as though she and Rob were being swept together in a torrent. And the rushing flow was hurtling them toward a surge of exploding energy. And then she did explode, unleashing a whirlwind of pleasure.

"Pamela," Rob cried out, as he reached his own climax. Then slowly, they fell to earth. Wrapping his arms tightly around her waist, he collapsed against her. As though together they had survived a joyous but cataclysmic experience, she enfolded him with her own arms. She felt as though her entire body were glowing, as though she would never be the same.

Propping himself up on an elbow, Rob looking down

at her face, studying its delicate features in the moonlight as though he'd never seen it before. "This felt so right," he whispered. "We're right together. Tell me you think so too, Pamela."

She didn't know what to think. She was capable only of feeling. "We're so different," she heard herself say.

Rob shook his head. "But that's what makes it so perfect. In our case opposites really do attract. It's like the moon's pull on the tides, the opposite poles of a magnet. Do you know John Donne's poem 'A Valediction Forbidding Mourning'? He draws an analogy between his relationship with his wife Anne and a draftsman's compass."

Pamela sorted through her memory, trying to recall the seventeenth century poets she'd read. But she couldn't bring the specific poem to memory.

Rob smiled and then began to quote:

> *"If they be two, they are two so*
> *As stiffe twin compasses are two,*
> *Thy soule the fixt foot, makes no show*
> *To move, but doth, if the 'other doe.*
>
> *And though it in the center sit,*
> *Yet when the other far doth rome,*
> *It leanes, and hearkens after it,*
> *And growes erect, as that comes home."*

As Pamela listened to his beautiful voice quoting the elegant words of love, she was very moved. But she wasn't sure how they applied to her relationship with him. "It's a wonderful poem. But it sounds like it has to do with his traveling and her staying at home."

Rob gently pushed a tendril of hair back from her forehead and leaned down to kiss the tip of her nose. "Very good, Miss Stewart. I can see that you were an excellent student in English Lit 201. But an image usually has more than one meaning—often several, in fact. Donne was talking about character as well as a specific situation. And that's what I was referring to."

Uncertainly, Pamela stared up at him through the shadowy light, wondering what exactly he meant.

"You think about it," he whispered, drawing her more tightly against his body. "But in the meantime, I'm tired of literary analysis. There are other things I'd rather do right now." Then he leaned over and kissed her.

5

Sunlight touched Pamela's eyelids and she awoke with a start. For a moment she was totally disoriented, her mind floundering for some sort of hold in what seemed like empty space. But gradually, bits of reality began to appear. The first thing she realized was that she was not in her own bed. The second was that a hair-covered arm was wrapped loosely around her naked breasts. She stared down at it in consternation, once again feeling disoriented as disconcerting technicolor pictures of the night before washed through her memory.

Glancing around wildly, she saw her and Rob's clothes tangled on the floor. Her sandals lay abandoned on the oriental rug, tipped on their sides like victims of an earthquake. And her blue dress was crumpled in a careless heap next to them.

Her emotional reaction to the scene was in direct opposition to what it had been the night before. Pamela was basically a very conservative person, and now that conservatism reasserted itself painfully. The night before had been a moon-silvered fantasy, but what had been romantic in moonlight seemed tawdry in the harsh sunlight. Again, she looked down at the arm around her breasts. After last night, what would she and Rob say to each other this morning? she wondered, frowning.

The past two days had been a wonderful, frivolous adventure—but such adventures inevitably come to an end. Now theirs was over, and prosaic reality had intruded. She found herself thinking back over their conversation at the Spanish restaurant. At the time, she'd admired Rob's devil-may-care attitude toward life. But now, in her chagrin over his easy conquest, she looked at it from a different point of view.

She and Rob were completely unalike. Last night that had spelled overwhelming sexual excitement. But once that momentary passion was gone, what would be left? They would fumble for words, knowing that their brief fling had no future. And a relationship without a future was no relationship at all. Distressed, Pamela swallowed. There wasn't enough depth in the relationship for anything more than a one-night stand, she told herself with a growing feeling of shame. How could she have been so heedless and foolish?

Moving very carefully so as not to awaken the sleeping man next to her, she slowly lifted Rob's arm from across her and slipped out from under it. She was suddenly so upset that she couldn't even bear to look directly at him. Once her feet were on the floor, she scurried to scoop up her clothes and dress. As she tiptoed around, she gave a quick glance at the bed to make sure Rob was still asleep. Looking like a sexy advertisement for bed linen, he was lying on his stomach with his face toward her. The sheet was down around his waist so that his powerful upper body was exposed. His closed eyelashes lay like silky dark crescents against his lean cheeks. And the expression on his sleeping face was one of satisfaction.

Turning away from the disturbing sight, Pamela hauled her dress over her head, stepped into her panties and moved silently out of the room carrying her shoes. In the living room she buckled her shoe straps, grabbed her jacket and looked around for her purse. So great was her hurry that she didn't even take time to check her hair in the mirror. She only hoped that she didn't have black smudges of mascara beneath her eyes and that everyone who looked at her wouldn't know in what way she'd spent the night.

Once outside Rob's townhouse, Pamela clattered down the street, anxious to get away as far as possible so that he wouldn't look out the window and see her. On Constitution Avenue she flagged a taxi and, ignoring the speculative look the driver shot her, gave him her address. As they rode through the streets, which at this early hour were just beginning to fill with commuters, she stared out blindly through the grimy window. Lost in her thoughts, she didn't see the imposing white marble Capitol, glass-walled Conservatory or any of the other government buildings that attracted tourists to Washington. Her mind was still trying to cope with the fragmentary scenes that were flashing chaotically through her head.

Her behavior had been so uncharacteristic that she felt almost as though she'd been bewitched. Maybe that wasn't so far from the truth. There really was an almost magical charisma about Robert Darcy. And she had fallen quite willingly under his spell. But now the enchanted night he'd spun around her was over. What was left was a strong feeling that she'd made an idiot of herself.

Just then the taxi pulled up to the curb in front of her townhouse. After rummaging in her purse, she hastily paid the man and rushed out in the hope of gaining her front door before any curious neighbors caught a glimpse of her. She just didn't want to have to manufacture explanations now.

Fortunately, she managed to get inside without encountering anyone. But once in the hall, she paused in front of the mirror on the wall to look at herself.

What she saw made her groan. Except for a few smudges of mascara, her face was devoid of makeup. Her hair looked like it had been through a high wind. Suddenly, despite herself, she smiled ruefully. The taxi driver must have known perfectly well that she wasn't on her way to work looking like this.

Running a hand through her tangled locks, she walked upstairs and headed for the shower. A few minutes later, as the needles of warm water cascaded over her body, she began once again to appraise the situation. One-night stands were certainly common enough among swinging Washington singles. However, she was anything but a swinger. What's more, this was no case of ships passing in the night. She was going to be seeing this man again—the next day at the festival, in fact.

The realization made her stomach knot. How would she handle that? Her cheeks went hot at the very thought. Needing something to do with her hands, she reached for the shampoo bottle and began to pour some of the rich liquid into the palm of her hand.

Then a disturbing new idea bubbled to the surface of her agitated mind. Her fingers stopped in the act of rubbing the shampoo into her scalp. Robert Darcy was a man who lived from grant to grant, and she was a grants administrator. What if he applied for money at the Harley Rutherford Foundation? She would be compromised.

Then an even worse thought struck her, one that made her go cold as ice in the warm spray. What if he'd deliberately seduced her because she might be of use to him? Such stories were not uncommon in her line of work. Robert Darcy was a dashingly handsome man. Yet, he'd lavished a great deal of time and attention on her the past two days. Pamela considered herself only passably good-looking. Objectively, it was hard for her to believe that Rob really found her as appealing as he'd claimed. The idea that he'd been merely cultivating her for some venal purpose was so horrifying that hot tears sprang to her eyes. She wrapped her arms around her body and shivered uncontrollably while the stream from the showerhead rinsed the soap from her hair.

But then she got hold of herself. That was a ridiculous notion. In fact, she was overreacting to this whole thing, she admonished herself sternly. He hadn't known what her job was when they'd first met. He was simply an attractive, virile man who'd charmed a vulnerable woman. Once more Pamela brought herself up short. This was ridiculous. Why was she thinking of herself as a victim? she scolded. Perhaps she'd done something foolish, but she was a grown adult and would take responsibility for it.

Pamela turned off the shower taps with a decisive twist, wrapped a fluffy rose-colored towel around her head, picked another one up and strode out into her bedroom. While she methodically dried herself she struggled to look at the situation dispassionately. There was no reliving last night's decisions. What was done, was done. It was what she did in the future that counted now. The only sensible thing was to terminate the romantic relationship with Robert Darcy. From now on there would be nothing of that nature between them.

But Pamela's rational conclusion was sorely tested an hour later. Dressed in shorts and a tee-shirt, she'd finished eating a bowl of cereal and was sipping at a cup of hot coffee, when her doorbell chimed. A dart of alarm struck her chest, and she straightened up in the pressed-back kitchen chair. Something told her that it was Rob. For a moment she sat as though turned to stone, unable to move or think what she should do.

The bell rang again, louder it seemed this time, and she got up from the chair and reluctantly walked out into the hall. Peering out through the peephole, she discovered that it was indeed Rob. He was pacing back and forth on her small stoop in a way that reminded her of the tigers they'd seen at the zoo two days earlier. Warily, she opened the door.

When it swung back, he stopped abruptly and stared at her. Always before Rob had been perfectly groomed. Now, he looked as if he'd dressed hurriedly. Wearing jeans and a pullover knit shirt, he hadn't bothered to shave and his crisp black hair looked rumpled.

"Why did you go off like that?" he blurted without preamble, pushing past her into the hall. As she quickly closed the door and turned, Rob faced her squarely, a hurt expression in his dark eyes. "I expected to wake up and find you beside me. But instead the bed was empty and your things were gone. You didn't even say good-bye or have the courtesy to leave a note. Why?"

For a moment Pamela was speechless. This accusation was the last thing she'd expected, and the irony of it struck her. It was as though they'd switched roles. She was tempted to say, "That's my line." But instead she heard the cool, efficient Pamela, the one who was a successful grants administrator, take over. "Would you like to come into the kitchen for a cup of coffee?" she invited.

Rob's face darkened, and his eyes flashed. Putting his hands on his lean hips, he snapped, "I didn't come here to kaffee-klatch, I came here to get some answers."

Pamela reddened. "Well, you're not going to get them in the hall. At least come into the kitchen so we can have a civilized conversation."

He stared at her, incredulous at the stand-offish tone

she was taking. Last night he'd thought they were Romeo and Juliet. But today she was the ice queen and he was nothing but a knave—a role he was not accustomed to and had no use for. With narrowed eyes, he followed her into the next room.

Once they were in the sunny kitchen, she turned again to face him. "Rob," she began, taking a deep breath, "it was a terrible mistake."

"Mistake!" His expression, she noted, seemed to grow even stormier. "What the hell do you mean by that?"

Pamela clasped her hands together tightly. Inwardly, she was trembling. But outwardly she strove to maintain a calm facade. "I mean that I behaved foolishly," she said, looking down at her clasped hands. "I was just caught up in the romantic atmosphere of the festival last weekend. I think we both were," she amended.

"But last night wasn't last weekend, and it had nothing to do with the festival."

Suddenly feeling the need for some kind of barrier between them, Pamela stepped to the other side of the table. Even in his present angry mood, Rob was overwhelmingly attractive to her. But she was determined to keep that hidden from him. "Oh, but last night had everything to do with the festival," she insisted. "I was still seeing you as that dashing, romantic figure, Robyn O'Dare. I was still caught up in the fantasy of it."

Rob exploded. "Romantic figure!" He leaned across the table and confronted her, his accusing face only a few inches from hers. "What are you telling me? Are you saying that I'm only a prop? A cardboard character trotted out to fulfill some sort of one-time fantasy? A puppet for your amusement?"

"No, no . . ." She put her hands out to stop the torrent of angry words. "It's not like that. It's just . . . we're oo difforent."

"So what?"

"So everything! We exist in different worlds. For a brief time we could come together at the festival. But though the character you're playing is very like you, the one I'm impersonating isn't really me." There was a knot in Pamela's stomach. "In real life we have nothing in common," she added, unconsciously wringing her hands. "And our relationship has no future."

Rob studied her with an exasperated expression. "You sound as if the goal of our seeing each other is to run off into the sunset and get married. What's wrong with our just enjoying each other as we are?"

Pamela crossed her arms protectively. Her explanations weren't coming out right, and she felt she was stepping deeper and deeper into quicksand. Perhaps it had sounded as if she were cold-bloodedly sizing him up for marriage and deciding he wouldn't do. "That's not what I meant," she said finally. "I meant that knowing our relationship has no future makes it seem so flimsy and unsubstantial. I guess I'm just not ready to settle for something like that."

"Flimsy!" Rob repeated. "Do you give all your relationships a grade? If memory serves, there was nothing flimsy about what happened last night."

Pamela bit her lip. "But last night was only physical," she protested, taking a step backward. "It was purely sex and nothing more."

Rob looked truly insulted. "Are you saying that what we had was nothing more than a one-night stand, then?"

Pamela's gaze dropped from his accusing stare. "I hate to label it that way. You're a special person, and I'd like to think we could go on being friends. But from now on, I don't want anything physical to happen between us."

The words sounded so final. As soon as they were out of her mouth, she realized that they weren't true at all. She wanted to be in Rob's arms again and was tempted, even now, to fly into them. But this time her common sense had to take precedence over her unruly emotions.

As though he'd read her mind, Rob said, "I don't believe you really mean that." Stepping forward, he took her shoulders between his hands and drew her close. Pamela fought with herself to resist. She knew if she yielded now, she would be lost.

Calling on all her reserves of strength, she steeled herself not to respond. When his lips closed over hers, he met only cool resistance. And though he used all of his considerable expertise to persuade her to respond, she was like a statue. But her icy exterior belied her inner turmoil. The Pamela behind that unfeeling facade was quivering with needs that were not to be fulfilled.

Rob couldn't be aware of this, however. He only knew that the warm and passionate woman he'd made love to the night before was now as unyielding as stone. What was going on? he asked himself. Women usually chased *him!* He'd never had one run away. And now, finally, he'd found this woman—so attractive, intelligent and passionate, yet so maddeningly indecisive. One minute he was sure she cared for him as much as he cared for her. Then the next minute she turned and pushed him away. He wasn't sure he wanted to keep playing this game.

Abruptly, he pulled away from her. "All right, if that's the way you want it," he said evenly, his deep voice suddenly edged with frost.

Then swiveling on his heel, he stalked from the room, and a moment later she heard the front door slam. Though she stood unmoving, she listened until she heard the throaty roar of his Volvo. When that, too, was gone, tears began to ooze from the corners of her eyes. An irrational sense of loss overwhelmed her. Collapsing in a kitchen chair, Pamela put her head in her folded arms on the table and wept uncontrollably. She hadn't meant for this to happen. She liked things neat and tidy, but all she'd succeeded in doing was creating a mess. Tomorrow she was going to be seeing Rob again at the Renaissance Festival. And there were five more weekends of the fair left. How was she going to face him?

That thought was very much in her mind as she opened her stand early the next morning. Glancing at the activity eddying around her, she dully took in the gaily colored costumes and high-spirited antics of the festival participants. Last week she had viewed this scene with such overflowing enthusiasm. Things had certainly changed since then—and all because of her own foolishness. What was supposed to have been a challenging, interesting sabbatical and an adventurous break from routine was turning out to be an ordeal. She glanced around warily, looking for Rob's athletic figure among the actors and craftspeople. He wasn't there, and she sighed with relief. She'd turned this light-hearted fling into turgid soap opera, she thought ruefully. She'd already spent one night tossing and turning while she thought up apologies to offer him. Now, in the light of day, they all seemed flimsy. What would she say to him? Better not worry about that now, she told herself.

She glanced at her watch. It was almost 10:30. The cider delivery man should have been here by now, she thought. Where was he? He never had replaced the turned cider the weekend before, and now she had only a couple gallons left to sell. When she'd called earlier in the week, he'd promised to make the delivery by nine in the morning. If he didn't come soon, she'd have a real problem, she worried, especially since eager fairgoers were already streaming across the field. Pamela put her hands on her hips and began to tap her toe on the hard-packed earth. She was depending on the cider for a good chunk of her income. Besides, she'd already paid the man for the jugs of hard cider, which were useless to her.

Just then her thoughts turned back to their original track. She spotted a tall, well-built swordsman in the distance, and her heart fluttered painfully in her chest. It was Rob, once more looking every inch the swashbuckling gallant who had caught her eye a week ago. At that moment he glanced up and across the meadow, and their gazes met. Though it was hard to tell at this distance, for a heartbeat she imagined that he looked uncertain. But then his athletic body seemed to stiffen, and he turned away and started to flirt with a wild-haired, buxom fishwife.

Was that how it would be for the next month? Pamela wondered. Would they just ignore each other and not speak? The thought was so bleak that Pamela's gaze dropped. She leaned over the counter and, with trembling hands, busied herself arranging her muffins. Though she tried not to look in Rob's direction, she did glance frequently at the corner of the field where the cider truck might make an inconspicuous entrance. But by 11:30 it still hadn't appeared, and she was beginning to feel a little desperate.

While a friendly woman from the next concession watched the stand, Pamela slipped away several times to try to call the cider mill. But the long distance number was always busy. When she came back from her last unsuccessful attempt, she stared glumly at the few inches remaining in her last jug. What would she do when it was gone?

"Why so downcast, milady?" a friendly voice queried.

Looking up, Pamela met the harlequin's clown-painted eyes. "Jake," she exclaimed, smiling. "It's great to see you again."

"Nice to see you, too," he returned. "But just a moment ago you were looking as though you had the weight of the world on your shoulders." Turning down the corners of his mouth and hunching his shoulders, he mimed an Atlas balancing an invisible burden.

Pamela laughed at him and shook her head. Then, sobering, she explained her dilemma.

Jake looked truly concerned. "That is a problem! Hmm," he said, cupping his hand around his sharp jaw. "Sounds like you're a lady in distress. Let me see if I can arrange a rescue mission."

Mystified, Pamela watched as he strode back down the field and disappeared into the throng. What had he meant? she wondered. But, only forty-five minutes later, she found out. A very unrenaissancelike truck from a local cider mill bounced up behind her stand.

"Oh, a cider truck!" Pamela cried, beaming from ear to ear as she ran toward the vehicle. Jake must have arranged for this, she thought, stopping alongside the cab. But when the door swung open, her smile faded to a look of confusion. Out leaped Rob in all his seventeenth century finery.

"I'm told there's a damsel in distress up here," he said with a faint smile.

Pamela clasped her hands in front of her bosom while she tried to sort out the situation. Obviously, Jake had told the handsome actor about her predicament. Though she hated being beholden to him, she certainly couldn't turn down the cider. She needed it too badly.

As Rob watched her equivocal expression, his uncertain smile vanished, and abruptly he turned away to open the back of the truck. Aware that she was not reacting properly, Pamela searched her mind for something to say that would ease the tension. But her brain wouldn't cooperate, and her tongue seemed to stick to the roof of her mouth. Just then Jake, who'd come up behind her, made the situation a little less awkward. Doing a surprisingly agile somersault for a man of his middle years, he grinned and shouted, "Hi ho Silver!"

Then, grabbing his throat in a pantomime of a man dying of thirst in the desert, he grated, "Quick, quick, cider for a dying man!"

Laughing, the three of them began unloading the jugs, and within fifteen minutes Pamela was more than adequately supplied with cider for the rest of the weekend. When everything was in place, she turned to thank her two rescuers, but they and the truck were already vanishing into the crowd.

Though Pamela had no more supply problems, and for the rest of the day she did a brisk business, she didn't enjoy her entrepreneurial success the way she'd hoped. As the afternoon wound down and the crowds drifted away, depression began to settle over her like the gathering dusk. While she made preparations to close up her stand, she glanced around surreptitiously from time to time. Though she told herself it was simply to assess the kind of day the other stands had had, it was really to look for Rob. While part of her was afraid he might approach, another part of her feared he wouldn't. When she saw him leave the grounds with his arm around a pretty blonde dressed as a lady in waiting, Pamela's heart sank.

How silly she'd been, she admonished herself. She'd known the cider was a peace offering, and she'd hurt him with her awkward, self-conscious response. Now, as she watched other people around her laughing and talking to one another, she felt more than ever like an outsider. If it weren't for her commitment to the fair's management, she thought, she'd be willing to lose her financial investment and pack up and leave.

"Oh, Pamela, this is stupid," she told herself out loud. "Stop behaving like a petulant child!"

"A petulant child? Hmph, I thought all those little urchins went home!" The exclamation came from a smiling older woman who was approaching her stand. She had shoulder-length brown hair streaked with gray, and wore large gold hoops in her ears. With her peasant blouse and long brown skirt trimmed with a bright red sash, the woman looked like a gypsy.

Pamela felt a bit embarrassed. "Oh, don't mind me," she said with a self-conscious wave of her hand. "I was just talking to myself."

"Oh, there's a remedy for talking to yourself," the woman chuckled, extending her hand. "It's called getting out and meeting people. Start with me. I'm Tess—better known as Tess the Turkey Leg Lady," she added, tossing her salt and pepper curls in the direction of the stand across the way.

"How do you do?" Smiling gratefully at the friendly, open-faced woman, Pamela politely extended her hand. "I'm Pamela Stewart and I'm pleased to meet you."

In answer, the gypsy woman wrapped her arms around Pamela's shoulders and hugged her. "Welcome to the Renaissance Festival! Is this your first time round?" Tess inquired.

Somewhat startled by this strange lady's enthusiastic greeting, Pamela pulled back. "Yes, it is, my very first."

Tess cocked her head and studied the young woman's fine features. "Get to know very many people yet, honey? I know you've met my old pal Jake because he told me what a lovely girl you are and said I should come over and introduce myself."

Pamela smiled. How like Jake it was to look out for her. He was really a very thoughtful man. "I've talked to a few people, but the only other person I've gotten to know is Robyn O'Dare," she volunteered, feeling a bit self-conscious about the admission, and hoping the slight flush on her cheeks wouldn't give her away.

Tess's round face lit up. "Ah ha, that Robyn O'Dare, he's a handsome devil. If I were a few years younger, I'd be out there chasing him myself right along with all the others."

Pamela lifted an eyebrow. "Others?"

Tess leaned a plump elbow familiarly on the counter. "Ah, yes. He's always a favorite with the ladies. And with looks like that, you can't really blame them, now, can you? I daresay he has his pick."

How true that statement was, Pamela thought. *She* certainly hadn't offered much resistance. And now all her suspicions about the man were being confirmed. The moment she'd seen him, she'd known he was a ladies' man and not for her. But despite all the warnings she'd issued to herself, she'd gone right ahead and practically fallen at his feet anyway.

"I daresay you're right," Pamela answered with feigned nonchalance. "He probably does have his pick. I suppose a lot of flirtation goes on at this festival."

"Oh, my dear!" Tess agreed with a wicked smile. "It's kind of a circus being here. We all want to frolic and forget the world out there. But what's the harm, I say? Everyone needs a little escape in their lives." She winked broadly.

Pamela searched her mind for a reply, but nothing surfaced. Fortunately, just then someone called Tess from across the way.

"Hold on to your horses!" Tess shouted and then turned back to Pamela. "Those boys," she said referring to her hired help, "can't do a thing without me. Well, dear, I hope to be seeing more of your pretty face as the weeks go by. Come across and sample one of my turkey legs tomorrow—on the house, of course!"

"Thanks, I will," Pamela called after her. But when the gregarious woman was gone, the smile once again faded from Pamela's features. Sighing, she began to carefully wrap and pack the muffins that were left. But her mind really wasn't on her task. Instead, it was on a dark, swashbuckling swordsman. She must be more than a casual conquest for him, she reflected. After all, he'd gone to all the trouble of getting the cider for her.

But the role of hero came so naturally to him. Maybe he just liked playing it.

Sighing again, Pamela stacked the last box in the refrigerator and closed the door. Was there any chance that she and Rob would at least renew their friendship? she wondered. Right now that didn't seem likely, but as time passed anything could happen.

As the weekends at the Renaissance Festival dragged by, however, Pamela saw Rob only from a distance. If he wasn't engaging in mock swordplay for the benefit of a cheering audience, or exchanging witty sallies with his redheaded opponent, he was flirting. Time after time, Pamela would look up from her stand to see Rob cupping the chin of some pretty visitor or stealing a kiss from a winsome Renaissance maid. Her only consolation was that he didn't seem to concentrate on any particular one, but favored all equally with his energy and charm. But if she'd had any doubts that the man was a flirt, they had been banished forever.

Several times, Pamela thought of approaching him. But then she'd see him smiling into another woman's eyes. To Pamela it almost seemed as if he were taunting her. Once again hurt and angry, she would turn away. And though it was unintentional, she even found herself flirting with Jake and hoping that Rob would notice.

Jake flirted right back, a knowing expression in his intelligent eyes. He'd told Pamela about Carolyn Bartlett, his girlfriend in Washington. Both he and Pamela knew they were merely playing a game; their relationship was strictly one of friendship. Several times she caught Jake studying her seriously when she'd been looking at Rob. He probably knew exactly what was going on, she thought. But he was too diplomatic to bring up the subject, and for that she was grateful.

Despite her unhappiness about the situation between herself and the swashbuckling swordsman, Pamela surprised herself by gradually getting into the whimsical mood of the fair. She met a number of interesting people, enjoyed playing her role as a maid of muffins. And I'm even going to make some pretty good money, she told herself proudly as she counted up her receipts on the next-to-last weekend of the fair. But a cloud hung over her success. What would happen after next week when the Renaissance Festival was over? she wondered. Would she ever see Rob again?

6

It was the last weekend of the fair and temperatures were topping an unseasonable one hundred degrees. Mopping her brow, Pamela watched with sympathy as Queen Elizabeth and her ladies-in-waiting paraded through the wooded glen and open fields in their heavy brocades and velvets and layers of petticoats. Pamela was uncomfortable enough in her own long homespun skirt and peasant blouse, but they must be about to faint. She felt even sorrier for the knights in armor who were scheduled to do battle later that afternoon. They probably felt like lobsters being broiled alive in tin cans.

Pouring herself a cup of cider to cool off, she swatted irritably at the horde of yellowjackets dive-bombing her glass. The annoying insects were clustered around all the food stands and garbage cans, but the sweet odor of the beverage she sold seemed to attract them like a magnet.

Pulling the hopsacking skirt away from her perspiring legs, Pamela took a seat on a bale of hay she'd placed behind the counter of the stand. Robyn O'Dare's performance was going on across the way, so there was a momentary lull in her business. His dueling show with his redheaded companion always drew a big crowd. Wistfully she glanced in the handsome actor's direction and then quickly looked away. This was probably the last time she would see the man who had briefly been her lover. After tonight everyone in the fair would pack up and head in separate directions. Many would go on to other festivals, but she would be returning to the routine of her busy life in Washington. How strange to think that today she was here perched on a bale of hay, wearing a long skirt and a wreath of flowers in her tawny hair, whereas tomorrow she'd be sitting in a board room discussing budgets and needs assessments, dressed in a dark suit with her hair neatly coiled at the nape of her neck.

Taking a sip from her cup, she asked herself how she felt about the fair's end. Financially, the sabbatical had been a success. She figured that when she dismantled her stand and counted up the receipts, she would have taken in half again as much as her original investment. However, she told herself, shifting her weight on the prickly straw, her purpose in being part of the festival had never really been making money. She'd come for the experience of being an entrepreneur in this fantasy setting and, even more importantly, for the escape. In that, the fair had only been partially successful.

She'd made some good friends here, especially Jake and Tess. But somehow, she admitted, she had never really felt a part of the free and easy group of crafts-people and thespians who were the regulars on the circuit. And the situation with Rob hadn't helped things, she told herself dryly.

As these thoughts ran through her head, from across the field she could hear the handsome actor's resonant voice and the crowd of happy fairgoers laughing at his witty sallies. What a mess she'd made of their relationship, she scolded herself. She'd handled it all wrong. Once more shifting uncomfortably on the straw, Pamela took another swipe at a bee and glared at it fiercely.

"Damn little pests," Tess commented, interrupting Pamela's musings. "They've been attacking my turkey legs too."

Looking up, Pamela gave Tess a smile. "This weather is unbelievable," she muttered. "It feels more like the beginning of August than the end of September."

Since first introducing herself the month before, the older woman had regularly visited Pamela's booth, filling her in on all the fair gossip—how the rent-a-wench was breaking up with the Sir Pikestave, how Yorick the Groveler had made Queen Elizabeth scream when he put a salamander in her goblet, and how the Pickle Merchant was hit on the head with one of his wares by an irate female customer who didn't take to his bawdy jokes.

Tess's stand had been a stop for everyone working at the fair, and as a result, she knew everything that was going on. And even though the older woman hadn't mentioned Rob's amours again, Pamela guessed that Tess probably knew about her own awkward relationship with the actor.

Now Tess was standing in front of her, hands on hips, grinning broadly. "What would you say to a nice, cool swim in a secluded river?" she asked.

"Oh," Pamela answered, wiping away a drop of sweat that was rolling down the side of her cheek, "right now that sounds heavenly." Lifting the wet hair off the nape of her neck, Pamela stood up and took a napkin from the counter to pat her damp skin dry. Before this day was out, she reflected, she would feel like a limp noodle.

"Well," Tess continued enthusiastically, "this is the last day of the fair. And we're having a big good-bye bash tonight behind my stand. Everyone's bringing food so there will be plenty to eat. Then afterward we're going to celebrate by going down to a spot I found last week for a moonlight swim."

"That sounds great, Tess. But I didn't bring my bathing suit."

The older woman laughed at that and waved a broad hand. "No need for bathing suits, honey. We're going to skinny dip."

Pamela's jaw dropped. "Oh," she finally managed. "I don't think so." The thought of Tess, as round as a queen bee, frolicking in the water with her pack of naked gypsies was a bit stunning to envision. Tactfully, Pamela suppressed a giggle. And she certainly couldn't picture herself in such an unlikely tableau.

Seeing Pamela's dumbfounded expression, Tess came around and patted her on the shoulder. "Look, with my figure," she said, running a hand over her generous hips, "if I don't worry, you certainly shouldn't. And anyway, it will be dark and no one will see anything." Giving the younger woman a considering look, she added, "We just want to splash around in the nice cool water and have some fun."

Pamela guessed that that was probably true. She didn't believe that Tess and her lighthearted friends went in for orgies. But still, the idea of skinny dipping, especially if Rob happened to be there, was disconcerting. She'd never done anything like that before. Frowning, she shook her head.

"Chicken," Tess teased. "The least you can do is come to the party and have something to eat. You can decide about the swimming later. We probably won't be heading toward the river until ten or eleven anyhow."

That sounded a little less threatening, and Pamela's frown softened into a shy smile. "Okay," she finally agreed, "the party sounds like fun. I'll try to make it."

"Promise you won't forget," Tess persisted.

"I won't."

After Tess left, Pamela fretted about the invitation. On the one hand, she was very tempted by the whole idea of ending her whimsical plunge into the fantasy of the fair with an experience to remember. She hated the idea of just quietly packing up her car and driving home.

On the other hand, she simply couldn't imagine herself nonchalantly skinny dipping with a pack of Renaissance gypsies. Just then a customer came up to buy cider, and Pamela filled a cup and gave him his change. But though she smiled prettily and chatted about the fair with him, her thoughts remained focused on Tess's party. When would she get the chance to do something like this again? she asked herself. Maybe when opportunities for adventures came your way, you had to seize them.

The argument was seconded by Jake, who stopped by her stand at closing time and encouraged her to attend the party. "It's always the biggest wingding of the season," the small man exclaimed. He jiggled his cap and bells and leered dramatically. "And if you come off to the river with us afterward, you'll be in for a real treat. Just imagine," he added in a voice filled with wonder, "Tess scampering through the trees like a generously endowed wood sprite. Believe me, it's a sight worth seeing."

Pamela had to laugh. Tess didn't seem to have any inhibitions at all. It must be wonderful to be like that, she mused, shaking her head. If only she could be that free. In this crowd, she always felt like Miss Goody-Two-Shoes or, Pamela reflected, the female version of Casper Milquetoast. Impatient with her own prudery, she folded her arms across her chest and tapped her foot.

"I'll come to the party," she finally promised the

jester before he headed off to give a final performance for the remaining fairgoers.

Closing up the stand on this last day took Pamela several hours. Not only did she have to clean up the premises, deal with the rental company who picked up her refrigerator and oven, but she had to dismantle the structure as well. The little bit of food and cider that was left over she had given away or packed to take to Tess's. So it wasn't until darkness had begun to fall that Pamela made her way toward the sounds of revelry coming from the woods behind Tess's stand. Fortunately, the dusk had brought a drop in the temperature. The air, while still hot and humid, was at least more tolerable. Clad in the jeans and blue gauze shirt that she'd changed into before she took down the booth, Pamela picked up her offerings of muffins and headed through the trees.

Beyond the lacy network of trunks and leafy branches she could see the dancing light of a bonfire and hear the sounds of high-spirited voices. Upon breaking through to the clearing, she came across one of Tess's vagabonds balanced on his haunches, turning a gyro on a spit over the flames. The juices dripping from the meat sizzled on the white hot coals, and the aroma of the highly seasoned food made Pamela's mouth water. It was obviously having the same effect on the merrymakers, who had gathered eagerly around the roast, expectantly clutching their empty paper plates.

The whole scene with its relaxed, friendly atmosphere made Pamela think of a fairy tale gypsy encampment. People were joking and bantering back and forth as they poured cups full of jug wine and scooped up food. There was certainly plenty to eat, she noted, looking down at the blankets spread with food. A hollowed-out watermelon fancifully carved like a Viking ship full of fruit graced the center of an old quilt laden with cheeses, pickles and breads. Platters piled high with crisply browned turkey legs sat on an old chenille bedspread bedecked with plates of raw vegetables and a variety of foods left over from the various stands.

One of the madrigal performers was singing as he sautéed mushrooms in a pan over the flames next to the gyro; and an acrobat brandished a bottle of retsina that he was offering to share with anyone who wanted to sample the strong, resinated Greek wine. The smell of the wood smoke mixed with the pungent odors of cooking food, the sounds of laughter and the shadowy, glimmering light among the tall trees had an odd effect on Pamela. All the childhood stories of Robin Hood and his band of merry men sprang to her mind, and she felt a shiver of excitement run down her spine. She was glad she'd come.

But then, in the flickering shadows, Pamela spotted a familiar lean figure wearing jeans and a shirt with rolled up sleeves. A little stab of anxiety hit her. It was Rob talking to Tess, and he appeared not to have yet seen Pamela. Suddenly a dozen panicky thoughts fluttered through her mind. Maybe she shouldn't have come to the party after all. She'd known that she would see Rob here, but she'd thought she could handle it. Yet now, as she felt her palms grow moist and a blade of fear edge up inside her, she wasn't so sure. Moving away and telling herself she would only stay long enough to be polite, she quickly turned in the direction of the food. Despite the weeks of longing for him and despite the thousands of mental rehearsals she'd held with herself, she wasn't ready to deal with Rob in person yet.

"Maid Pamela!" Jake shouted as she placed her offering of muffins on the food blanket.

She waved and smiled as the jester, now clad in cutoffs and tee-shirt, came up to her and proffered a paper cup filled with red wine. Taking it from his hands, she thanked him. But her appreciation was for more than the wine; it was for the welcome diversion from her turbulent emotions that he provided.

"Great party," Jake commented, as they stood there balancing their cups and watching the activity surrounding them. "Say, while you're trying the wine, let me stuff a pita bread for you with some of that meat," he offered like an attentive host. "I think it's about ready."

As he went to get the gyros, Pamela took a large swallow of the wine. Her throat had become so parched from working in the heat of the day that she found herself almost gulping the smooth liquid. By the time Jake had returned and handed her a serving of the Greek food, she had drained her cup and was feeling a bit woozy.

"Mmmm!" she exclaimed as she bit into the half circle of thin bread stuffed with the spicy blend of lamb and beef. As she munched the highly seasoned sandwich and sipped a second and a third glass of wine, she forced herself to forget Rob and chatted with Jake and a few of the festival regulars. They laughed over some of the mishaps they'd encountered during the fair's six-week run and shared tales of difficult customers. Even the muffin debacle was funny in the retelling and her appreciative audience laughed as she described the shambles Rob's boot had left of her cakes. Secretly, she'd been afraid she'd have little to say to the party-goers, but to her surprise, the conversation flowed easily.

It was almost ten o'clock when Rob strolled up and joined the group. As his tall handsome form entered their little circle, Pamela's heart seemed to skip a beat. Though she'd been almost constantly aware of him during the past few weeks, they'd hardly exchanged a word since the day he'd solved the cider shortage. But now, mellowed by the wine, she stood her ground and said a cordial "hello." Raising an eyebrow slightly, he returned her greeting and fell into easy banter with the group. However, as if on cue, the others soon drifted away, and Rob and Pamela found themselves alone with each other.

For a few minutes, they stood in awkward silence watching the rest of the party. "How are things going with you?" Rob finally asked, searching her face.

Pamela's gaze quickly dropped from his. She felt as nervous and uncertain as a teenager on a first date with the boy she had a crush on. "Just fine. I'm not going to lose any money. As a matter of fact," she added with a touch of pride, "I made quite a bit."

"Well, you certainly looked like you were doing well enough whenever I glanced your way."

She eyed him with a startled expression. He'd been watching her? Her cheeks reddened with surprised pleasure. How often had his eyes strayed in her direction? she wondered, still doubting that it could have been anywhere as frequently as hers had gone to him.

"I've missed you," he added abruptly.

As she studied his face in the shadows, she thought back to all those times when she'd considered making some sort of peace offering. But at the last moment, afraid to appear foolish, she'd always backed out. Now that he'd made the first move, however, it seemed the right time for her to express her regrets. "Rob," she began hesitantly, "I never did thank you properly for helping me with the cider." She grimaced. The words seemed so stilted and hollow, not at all what she'd meant them to be.

Before she could rephrase them, he'd answered quietly, "I was glad to help."

She was taken aback by how subdued he seemed—not at all like his usual exuberant self. Suddenly it was urgent that she make him understand just how bad she felt about her foolish behavior. She looked him in the eye.

"Nevertheless, it was awfully good of you to go through all that trouble for me, especially," she went on with her apology, "considering what happened between us last time."

A strained silence stretched between them. "You know, Pamela," he finally said, taking one of her slender hands in his, "I'm still not really too sure what happened last time."

Pamela struggled to frame a reply, but so intense had her feelings grown that she could only stare mutely at him. Tess's ringing voice broke the awkward moment.

"Time to get the show on the road," the turkey leg proprietor boomed out in her best Ethel Merman style. Making her way among the happy crowd, she thumped on a tambourine, herding a gaggle of merrymakers through the woods toward the spot where the vans and pickup truck were parked. Rob was still holding Pamela's hand as Tess gave them a playful shove on the shoulders. "Come along, children," she clucked at them. "Get a move on."

Immediately, Pamela found herself swept up in the wave of people heading off for the moonlight swim. And a few minutes later she was jostling along with Rob, Jake and a singing throng in the back of a pickup truck.

It seemed like very little time had passed before their truck and the two vans of Renaissance folk that followed were pulling off the main highway onto a dusty country lane. As the vehicles bumped along the rutted road, the partygoers in the truckbed joked and laughed merrily. Slightly tipsy from the wine and jubilant camaraderie, they began teasing one another outrageously.

"Hey, Tess, I'm sure looking forward to seeing you in all your bountiful glory," the Pickle Merchant cried out, making an expansive gesture with his arms. "You are going skinny dipping, too, aren't you?"

"Sure am," she said, archly. "How about you?"

"I wouldn't deprive you girls of such a vision of grandeur," he joked.

Tess shot him a derisive glance and then, looking him up and down, quipped, "I seriously doubt you've got much glory to display." She poked her guffawing inquisitor in his stomach. The merrymakers in the truck roared at that and the good-natured ribbing continued. Gales of guffaws shook the truck as others got into the act.

"I don't know about the rest of you blackguards, but I'm looking forward to a swim with some of the pretty ladies in their birthday suits," another voice cried out. It was Yorick the Groveler.

Jake answered that one. "But they're not looking forward to swimming around with you, Yorick. You haven't seen water since we skinny dipped at last year's festival."

"Grovelers aren't supposed to take baths," Yorick replied with mock dignity. "Dirt is part of our profession."

Cheers greeted this rejoinder. But though Pamela smiled along with the shadowy faces in the crowded darkness, a knot was tying itself in her stomach. She couldn't help wondering what was going to happen once they reached the water's edge. Her eyes turned toward Rob's profile. He was grinning, thoroughly enjoying the lively banter. Occasionally, he tossed in a remark of his own and the crowd whooped. As the conversation swirled past Pamela at a dizzying speed, she realized that she was the only one not tossing off one-liners. But she didn't know how to join their fast-paced exchanges. They all seemed to have a sixth sense about what would amuse one another, and witty sallies whizzed back and forth like gunfire in a western shootout.

Pamela wove her hands together in her lap. She couldn't help feeling anxious about her own role.

Despite her involvement with the fair, she was still so unlike these people. Yet, she told herself, they'd all been very friendly. If she didn't fit in, it was simply her fault, not theirs.

Still, she suspected that she'd grow even more uncomfortable when they arrived at the river. Earlier, as she'd climbed into the truck, she'd promised herself that she'd go along and watch from the sidelines. But now Pamela wasn't happy with that. How would it seem if everyone else was cavorting around naked and there she was, sitting on the banks like a voyeur? It would appear that she was deliberately setting herself apart and that she was either too prudish or too superior to join in the free-spirited festivities.

Meanwhile, as all these troubling thoughts skidded around in her mind, Jake and Rob were on either side of her, exchanging witticisms. "Are you going to wear your polka dot Jockey shorts?" Rob asked the jester.

"No, just my cap and bells, strategically placed, of course," Jake retorted merrily.

Just then Tess leaned forward from the opposite bench and nudged Pamela on the knee. "I'm so glad you decided to take the plunge with us, dear." She chuckled encouragingly. "That water's going to feel soooo delicious," the heavy-set woman added, opening her arms in an embracing motion. "Especially after riding with such a crew and all this hot air blowing about." She rapidly opened and closed her fingers in imitation of moving mouths.

"I don't know," Pamela replied, with a little nervous laugh. "I think I'll just get my feet wet."

"Will they be *naked feet?*" Yorick the Groveler demanded.

Pamela couldn't help laughing. "Oh, of course not," she replied with dramatic primness. "I'm going to wear my shoes. No, maybe I'll wear my hiking boots." To her surprise and pleasure, the others chuckled at her retort and she earned a chorus of "huzzahs" from the troupe. But, along with the cheers, she heard Rob's voice in her ear.

"Spoil sport," he teased. "I won't allow you to ruin your shoes or your boots. I'll help you take your clothes off," he offered.

Tess, ignoring Rob's joshing and seeming to recognize the fear behind Pamela's little joke, said quietly, "Oh, once you're there, you'll forget all about being self-conscious. You'll be splashing around with all the rest of us and having a marvelous time."

Pamela wasn't at all sure of that, but she didn't have much longer to think about it because a moment later the truck and the vans had pulled off the side of the lane and rumbled to a stop. After everyone had clambered out, she looked around and saw nothing but dark woods only faintly illuminated by moonlight. In the distance, she heard the sounds of rushing water.

"Light the lanterns," someone shouted. "The path is just on the other side of that big pine tree."

With careful footsteps, she followed Jake and Rob down a winding path strewn with rocks and tree roots. "Watch your footing," Tess called out as one of their company took a tumble.

"I'm glad Daniel Boone didn't have you leading him through the wilderness, especially with your stomach full of retsina," said Jake, looking down at Yorick, who had somersaulted down the steep path and now lay sprawled in the leaves. "The borders of the United States would end at Cumberland, Maryland."

"Ah, but Daniel Boone probably didn't have half as good a time," the Groveler shot back, standing up and brushing off his jeans.

It was a good ten minutes before the little band finally reached the water, and all that time, along with her fears about skinny dipping, Pamela kept worrying about snakes and poison ivy. "I guess I'm just not pioneer stock," she muttered under her breath as she picked her way down a steep part of the trail. Sliding on an incline, she grabbed on to a tree branch to keep from falling.

"Well, I always preferred beauty and brains to physical prowess—or at least some forms of physical prowess," Rob retorted.

Pamela smiled at his flippant but flattering remark. However, she couldn't help feeling inadequate to this little midnight escapade. Stumbling around the woods in the middle of the night definitely wasn't her forte. Nevertheless, when they finally reached the banks of the river, she forgot about rashes, reptiles, insect bites and falling on her face. Standing on a little clearing at the edge of the woods, she drew in her breath and gazed at the vista. The river was wide here and the moon lit its smooth surface with a silvery sheen. It was an ideal place for a midnight frolic, she thought. Several large boulders jutted out into the dark river, making natural perches for getting into the water. Though the water was high because of rain earlier that week, the current looked gentle. Aside from the quiet lapping of the river and the muffled laughter of the Renaissance gypsies, the only sounds were a muted chorus of frogs and katydids. After the hurly-burly of the festival with its heat, dust and crowds, this was like stepping into another, far more serene world.

Hanging back in the shadow of a tree, Pamela waited to see what would happen. Little shivers of nervousness ran up and down her backbone as she watched the others. If she had imagined that they would feel some discomfort about peeling off their clothes en masse, she found she was quite mistaken. After setting down lanterns and sticking their toes in the water to check out the temperature, the shadowy figures of the celebrants, Rob among them, began discarding jeans, shirts, underwear and shoes. No one seemed the least self-conscious, and Pamela began to feel quite foolish about her own qualms. She peered into the uncertain light. Tess had been right about not being able to see much. In the moonlight, the glimpses of pale bodies that Pamela caught were indistinct. And once in the river, the gypsies were invisible except for their heads. Pamela moved out from the shadows, edging closer to the riverbank where she found a seat on a rock and removed her sandals. When her feet were bare, she dangled them over the edge into the cool water.

As she sat there, watching the group plunge into the river, she was reminded of gracefully leaping fish. And although some of the swimmers' remarks were ribald, the atmosphere was lighthearted. It was as though everyone had shed the cares of adulthood with their clothes and had retreated to the innocence of childhood. Splashing and laughing, they doused each other and swam back and forth across the pool formed by the rocks in this crook of the river.

Pamela was beginning to feel very conspicuous, huddled by herself on a rock. It was like being a wallflower at a junior high school dance—worse, because she had only herself to blame for being out of it. She tried to pick out Tess and finally spotted her bulky shape. She and the Groveler were busy dunking each other. Suddenly Pamela wanted to join the merriment, but she noted ruefully that she'd missed her chance. The time to remove her clothes had been when everyone else was doing it. She looked around her and saw no one on the banks. They were all in the river. If she took her clothes off right now, she'd feel as though she were doing a striptease.

In the festive confusion, Rob had disappeared into the water without her noticing, but now he surfaced a few feet away from her. She heard his deep voice and saw a muscular arm wave to her. "Come on, the water's great!"

She surveyed the scene longingly. The river did look coolly inviting, and her skin still felt sticky in the humid air. Maybe she'd feel more comfortable, she reasoned, if she slipped off her things in the shadow of the big old tulip tree nearby. She glanced around her again. Anyhow, no one, except Rob seemed to be paying much attention to her, and he'd already seen her naked.

"Come on, killjoy," Rob said, flicking a silvery spray of water in her direction. "I won't look, if that's what's bothering you." Making good on his word, he turned his back and began swimming away from her.

"Okay, I'll be right there," she called after him. Picking up her sandals, she moved toward the shelter of the broad tree, put down her shoes and began unsnapping her jeans. Damp from sweat, they fit snugly and were difficult to wriggle out of. Looking around apprehensively, she struggled from them and then boldly stepped out of her panties. In the next moment, she'd pulled her shirt off, unhooked her bra and left her clothes in a pile at the foot of the tree. Feeling exposed despite the darkness, she picked her way quickly along the rock-strewn bank, intent on diving into the water.

Once it had enveloped her sticky body, she sighed with pleasure. Enjoying the velvety slide of the water along her skin, she took a couple of strokes. Never before had Pamela swum naked. How unexpectedly free she felt! The river seemed to caress her breasts and hug her flanks. She was so caught up in the liberating sensations that the sounds of the others frolicking further up the river seemed to fade into the distance.

The spot where she'd entered the water was relatively secluded and as she turned over on her back and stared up at the moon and stars, she felt like Eve in Paradise. How brightly the stars glittered in the velvety sky. As she floated, her eye traced the line of the Big Dipper and she wondered if the reddish-looking glow above her was Mars. Turning her face toward the bank, she saw what looked like moving stars among the trees. Fireflies, she thought with a little shiver. How lovely! The scene seemed so magically beautiful that she almost expected to see the fairy king and queen from *A Midsummer Night's Dream* step out from the shadows and go romping through the trees.

A splashing noise broke into her reverie, and she heard Rob's deep voice chuckle. "So, Queen Titania," he said, "you finally decided to join us mere mortals."

Pamela laughed delightedly, but an instant later, realizing that her breasts were exposed to view, she rolled over in the water. "How did you know that I was thinking about *A Midsummer Night's Dream*? Are you a mind reader?"

"No, I'm afraid mind reading's not in my repertoire, but," he added, coming closer to her, "it's only natural to think of Shakespeare's romantic fantasy in this wooded setting." As he spoke, his eyes traveled appreciatively over the graceful line of her naked back. "This place does seem enchanted, and now that you're down here with me," he added, in his rich voice, "it's doubly so."

To hide her reaction to the warmth in his voice, she gave him a playful splash. "Flatterer," she teased, forgetting her self-consciousness.

Pamela laughed at him when he splashed her in retaliation, but a moment later her expression sobered as he drew nearer to her, put a hand on her shoulder and said, in a serious voice, "It's been a long time, Pamela. And I've had a lot of sleepless nights." He massaged her shoulder tenderly and brushed it with his mustache. "I've already said it once before, but let me repeat myself. I've missed you."

Pamela quivered as a pang of longing stirred deep within her loins. Rob wasn't the only one who'd had some sleepless nights. Feeling her cheeks go warm and not knowing how to respond to his overture, she rolled to her side and slowly swam toward the deeper part of the river. Rob followed along, effortlessly parallelling her course.

As they glided through the water he admired the sleek shape of her body. "I've always wanted to swim with a water sprite," he told her. For several moments they moved down the river silently, the only sound coming from the motion of their bodies cutting through the water. The quiet and the darkness heightened Rob's sense of unreality. He couldn't believe this was happening—certainly not after the cider incident when she'd seemed so cold. He had feared that he and Pamela would never be together again. But now, he began to hope there was a future for them, after all.

Unaware of his thoughts and distracted by her own desires, Pamela reached for the bottom with her feet and wiggled her toes in the soft mud. Because of her sudden stop, Rob drifted into her and suddenly she felt his arms go around her naked hips. The contact sent a bolt of electricity up Pamela's spine and she quivered. Automatically, she tried to pull back, but the current was against her. And when Rob's arms didn't release her, she found herself drifting against his hard masculine body. With a shock of pleasure, she realized how much she liked being held by him and how much she'd missed him. They'd spent so little time together, merely a few days; but that time had been charged with intensity. He'd made a place for himself in her life, and during the weeks they'd been apart, she'd felt the emptiness.

His next words echoed her thoughts. "Lord, this feels good, Pamela," he said, as he stroked her smooth shoulders. "You're so soft. It's been hell these last few weekends at the festival, seeing you and yet knowing you wanted me to keep my distance." His lips nuzzled her ear gently, causing tremors to ripple through her limbs. Their bodies were pressed tightly to each other now, and even in the cool water, Pamela felt the rising heat of his arousal. She knew that if she was going to stop this, she should pull away now, but she didn't want to. It was as though all her reasons for avoiding him were dissolving in this enchanted river. Though she knew her earlier reasons for cutting off the relationship had been compelling, somehow, in the black magic of this starry night, she couldn't seem to remember what they were.

"Oh, Water Witch, you must know what charms you're using to imprison me," Rob said huskily, breaking into her confused thoughts.

"What happened to Maid Muffin?" Pamela whispered in his ear before nibbling on the lobe.

"I suspect she's only a front for the sorceress who's weaving a spell on this poor mortal." He pulled her even closer to him and she gasped with delight. "You know that I want to make love to you," he whispered in a thickened voice while her arms twined around his neck. "But this just isn't the right time or place."

Just then the shouts from the gypsies further up the river grew more boisterous, proving the validity of Rob's point. "I think we're about to have company," he said, reluctantly drawing away from her.

"Ah ha, there's Rob!" Pamela recognized the blustery voice of Brian Bliss, Rob's partner and redheaded opponent. "We'd practically dredged the river for you. We thought for sure you'd floated out to the ocean." Suddenly the actor stopped short. Apparently he had just noticed that Rob was not alone. "Oh, a thousand pardons," he said quickly and in a more polite tone, as he squinted in the darkness.

"We were just coming back to join you," Rob fibbed. Taking Pamela's hand, he began to lead her back up the river toward the group. But the spell was broken and she started to pull away, still not really wanting to splash around naked with the others. "I think I'll go get dressed now. My clothes are just up by that tree," she said, nodding in the direction of the spot where she'd left her things.

Rob, however, wasn't going to let her escape. He didn't want to take a chance on losing her again. And if she went off now, he might lose her for good. Determined, he laced his fingers in hers and matched her short steps as she waded toward the bank. "I'm coming with you."

7

Just as Pamela was pulling on her jeans, the others began trooping out of the water. Rob left her alone a few minutes to join them and find his own clothes which were strewn among the other garments in helter-skelter piles on the bank. As the gypsies scrambled to pick out their things from those of their comrades there was a good deal of boisterous laughter.

"Hey, what do you think you're doing, trying to put on Tess's skirt?" Jake shouted at the Groveler, who was looking for his pants amid the tangle of clothing. Pamela, from her isolated perch, heard shrieks of mirth.

Giggling, Pamela hastened to tuck in her blouse and strap on her sandals. Then she twisted her hair, wet from the river, into a knot at the top of her head, securing it with bobby pins from the pocket of her jeans. When she was finished, she took a deep breath and stepped out from the shelter of the tulip's branches. She felt a bit embarrassed about being too shy to join the other fairworkers earlier and wondered if anyone had noticed that she'd slipped into the water by herself. Of course, she thought, a secret smile playing about her lips, she hadn't been alone for long. Had anyone taken note of that? And would they tease her about it if they had?

Her speculations were soon answered by the Groveler. "Ah ha," he shouted. "It's our modest muffin maid." He poked at Rob, who was now fully dressed, and leered. "You rascal. I saw you slip out to join her in the river. Just what were you two up to anyway?" Grinning broadly, he gave Rob another poke. "As if I didn't know."

Pamela's cheeks went hot in the darkness, and she touched her palms to them. Everyone else was romping about with such abandon and here she was again behaving like someone's prim and proper spinster aunt.

Rob, however, merely laughed off the Groveler's remarks. "You're just jealous," he teased Yorick. "The closest you ever get to a lady is touching her hem."

"An insult!" Yorick cried with good humor. Then grabbing two sticks from the ground, he tossed one at Rob and shouted "en guarde." The handsome actor seized the "weapon" and, in the next moment, the two were shouting inventive insults at each other as they dueled back and forth along the riverbank to the sound of the group's encouragement.

"Defend my honor," shouted Tess, pointing at the would-be macho duelist. "That blackguard tried to steal my clothes!"

Momentarily swept up in this festive make-believe, Pamela forgot her chagrin and cheered loudly along with the others. The mock battle ended a minute later when Yorick's stick broke and he threw himself at Rob's feet, comically begging for mercy while his handsome opponent stroked his chin, pretending to be considering clemency. Tess recommended dunking as a fit punishment.

Obligingly, Rob tossed the offending Groveler into the river while the group, led by Tessie, applauded heartily. After hoisting their compatriot out of the river and giving him a few pats on the back, the gypsies began straggling through the woods to where the vans and truck were parked. As Pamela trudged along, Rob came up beside her and once more took her hand. "This little moonlight adventure wasn't so bad, was it?" he asked, bringing her fingers to his mouth and dropping kisses on their tips.

"No," she managed huskily, "it wasn't bad at all. I'm not totally sure I recognize this Pamela," she murmured, leaning against his shoulder for a moment, "but whoever she is, she's having a good time."

Rob chuckled. "This is just another side of you. All you have to do is give it a chance," he said as they resumed walking.

While they started up the steep path, she considered his words. This night seemed so unreal to her, much like the first evening when she'd met Rob and they'd picnicked under stars. She had lost herself in a fantasy world that night, too. What was it about this man that broke down all her barriers? Most of her adult life she'd kept a fence around her emotions. But it had been a struggle to maintain any defense against this man. In fact, much to her surprise, tonight she found that she was sorry their interlude in the river had come to an end so quickly.

Rob was apparently thinking along the same lines. "I wish we had been all alone in the river," he whispered in her ear. "I'll probably never have another chance to make love to a gorgeous water sprite. Or will I?" he added, stroking the crown of her still damp hair.

Pamela shivered at his touch and wondered how to

answer the question. Instead of replying, she nuzzled her head against his shoulder once more and then pulled away as they reached the clearing where the truck stood.

Realizing that the end of the fair had really come, the little band broke up and piled quietly into the vehicles. As they moved out, Pamela felt a tear slide down her cheek. Now that she'd finally become somewhat comfortable with this strange, charming collection of people, she didn't want the fantasy to end.

In contrast to the boisterous trip out, the ride back was sedate. It was late, almost two o'clock in the morning, Pamela guessed. As they bumped along, some of the merrymakers snoozed, while others exchanged plans for upcoming festivals in faraway states. Leaning against the crook of Rob's arm, Pamela listened to this talk of fairs, caravans and constant travel. What would it be like to lead this gypsy life? she wondered once again. Her time at the fair had been exciting for a few weekends, but she hadn't actually lived with these free-spirited vagabonds, and she couldn't picture herself being comfortable, leading such a makeshift, hand-to-mouth existence. She was still mulling this over as the pickup and the vans behind it shuddered to a halt. Suddenly the fair was all over, much too quickly for Pamela. Everyone climbed out, hugged and said their good-byes before drifting off in different directions.

When they were alone, standing in the woods by the side of the truck, Pamela and Rob looked at each other. Was this the last time she would see him? she wondered. She didn't want to say good-bye, especially not after what had happened in the river, but she didn't know what else to do.

"I suppose I should go to my car now," she finally murmured, casting her eyes downward.

Rob, however, had no intention of letting her go. Stepping forward, he caught her hands, and she knew she wouldn't try to break free. Through the moonlight filtered by the network of branches, she could only see the outlines of his features, but she could feel his gaze on her, warm and intent. "Don't leave yet, Pamela. Please," he begged her.

"I won't," she found herself whispering. Was that really her voice quivering in the darkness? She hardly recognized it. Her hands trembled in his. Where was the resolve that had given her the strength to refuse him a few weeks back? It had vanished like a puff of smoke in the witchery of this late summer night. Her whole body ached with desire, and she knew she wanted him as much as he wanted her.

"Come with me," he said, and Pamela mutely followed. He was leading her toward the part of the forest where the performers and craftspeople camped. Pamela had never ventured back through this area. She'd either been too busy or too shy to invite herself into the Renaissance gypsies' private world. As she and Rob picked their way along the dirt path to the secluded settlement, she glimpsed temporary shelters of tents, old converted school buses, vans and cars parked among the shadows of the trees. Some of the makeshift encampments were illuminated by the flickering light of small bonfires around which festival performers gathered in small, hushed knots. But for the most part, the camps sat dark and silent.

"Looks like most people are asleep," Rob said in a low voice.

She nodded. "Will all this disappear tomorrow?"

He put his arm around her shoulder. "Yes, in the morning they'll all be packing up to go, and these woods will be quiet until the festival performers descend on them next year. It's sort of like Brigadoon, where the village vanishes, only to rise out of the mist every now and then."

"Yes, but it's sad," said Pamela.

"Why?"

"Because good-byes and endings are always sad."

Rob turned her toward him. "Well, then let's not have either." He bent down and gently claimed her lips with his. "Agreed?" he asked, brushing his mustache back and forth in a persuasive, tantalizing motion.

In response, Pamela pressed herself closer to him and reached up to wind her arms around his neck.

For a long moment, they stood beneath the star-strewn sky, oblivious to everything around them. "Oh, Rob," she breathed, caressing his face with her lips. She ran her hand over his fine brow and stroked his temple. She could feel the curling hair that framed his strong chiseled features, and she rubbed one finger across the silky sweep of his mustache. "Mmmm," she murmured as a ripple of desire welled up in her breast.

"Are you partial to men with mustaches?"

"I never was before," she answered, running her tongue along the tips of his mustache hairs. "I guess you made a convert." Again, her lips met his, and he pulled her hips against him as he explored her with his questing tongue.

When he finally lifted his head from hers, she asked, "Are you going back to Washington tonight?" She ran her hand down the back of his neck, hoping desperately that his answer would prompt an invitation to his house or hers.

"No, I have a place to stay here."

Pamela's eyebrows lifted. She couldn't picture Rob, who seemed to do everything with such elegance, making do with a tent. Was he staying here with someone? A sudden dart of jealousy went through her, breaking the tender mood, and she abruptly pulled back from him. So often during the last few weekends she'd seen him flirting with other women, particularly the buxom fishwife. No matter how taken she was with Rob, she refused to be part of a harem. "Are you camping out?" she found herself asking a bit stiffly.

Rob chuckled and pulled her close to him again. "I have deluxe accommodations. Would you care to see them?"

Pamela sighed with relief. If he was inviting her to inspect the place where he stayed, he couldn't be rooming with another woman. "I'd love to," she replied, knowing full well, and not caring, that this was a proposal for more than a tour.

Side by side, arms around each other's waists, they strolled further along the path. Pamela's heart was beating wildly as she looked up at the stars twinkling down on them. Her hand rested on Rob's ribs, so that she could feel the warmth of his body and his strong, steady breathing. The rise and fall of his chest had quickened somewhat, she thought, and she knew that he was feeling the same excitement that was heightening all her own responses.

A few moments later, he stopped and pointed out a large boxy shape among the trees. "That's the Sherwood Forest Hilton where I'm hanging out these days."

Pamela squinted into the darkness and then laughed as she realized what he was talking about. "What is it? Is it a van?"

"Yes, but no ordinary one," Rob said, holding up a finger and leading her toward the vehicle. "This is a van extraordinaire."

Pamela's eyes widened. It was difficult to see much in the dark, but in the wavering light of the moon, she could make out swirling shapes on the truck's paneled outside. On closer inspection, she noted that the van was covered with what she guessed were psychedelic paintings. Somehow she couldn't picture Rob driving around Washington in this rather adolescent fun-mobile. "Is this yours?" she finally asked, her voice rising in astonishment.

Rob shook his head in the negative. "No, it was lent to me by a musician friend who's traveling in Europe for the summer. Too bad it's not light out. You're missing the full impact. Its facade is done in a tasteful, sophisticated blend of neon pink, tomato red, chartreuse and gold glitter."

Pamela smiled at the image that description conjured up, yet at the same time, she couldn't help feeling relieved. Rob continually surprised her, but his owning this garish truck would have been more than she could handle.

Her amusement increased when Rob slid open the van's side door, flipped on the lights and invited her in. As she peered inside, Pamela's jaw dropped. Compared to the interior, the outside of the van was modest. Red plush carpeting covered the walls, floors and ceiling. Huge purple velvet pillows dripping with orange ball fringe lay pushed against the walls, and from the ceiling dangled a rice paper lantern—one of those ones printed in bright-colored patterns to resemble Tiffany glass.

"Come step into my parlor," Rob murmured in the same tone old movie villains used to invite innocent heroines to the Casbah.

Pamela cast her host a sideways look. "That sounds more like a threat than an invitation," she teased. Nevertheless she hoisted herself into the van and stood arms akimbo surveying its flamboyant decor. "Who was the decorator?" she inquired. "Genghis Khan?"

"Gypsy Rose Lee," Rob tossed over his shoulder. "House rules—you have to take off your shoes so as not to sully its scarlet beauty."

Pamela laughed, slipped off her sandals and wiggled her toes in the thick carpet. Rob had already done the same.

"Feels good, doesn't it? Sort of like walking on a red sea. But the air in here," he added, wiping a drop of perspiration from his forehead, "doesn't feel so great. I wanted to invite you to the crimson palace, not the red hot inferno." Pushing back the ruby velour curtains and sliding open the side windows, he announced, "I'm going to see if I can get things cooled down." After climbing over the pile of pillows, he went to the front of the van and she heard him rustling around.

While he was gone, Pamela unpinned her hair and shook it free, running her hands through the nearly dry strands. Then she continued her inspection. A tiny closet door with a MOTHER EARTH calendar caught her eye first; she supposed Rob kept his clothes there. A little stove and sink unit sat off to one side. The rest of the interior, though garish beyond the realm of bad taste, was surprisingly uncluttered. The only sign of Rob's transient presence was a few paisley-printed Indian sheets rumpled in a corner along with several assorted magazines. She glanced curiously at their covers, expecting in this setting to see *Mother Jones, Rolling Stone* or some other counterculture publication. Instead, she was surprised and rather pleased to find *The Shakespeare Quarterly, Harper's* and the Style section of what was now yesterday's *Washington Post.*

Suddenly Pamela was startled by the sound of gentle music surrounding her. She stood still, taking in the delicate strains of Renaissance recorders whose notes seemed to wrap her in the same fragile mood she'd experienced earlier in the river. Hugging her hands across her chest, she glanced up, noting the source of the sound—four speakers mounted in the ceiling, one in each corner. Just then a grating noise brought her attention to the center of the plush-covered top of the van where a plexiglass bubble was sliding open to the stars. Placing one hand on her hip, she shook her head in disbelief. This truck was outfitted like a desert sheik's harem, minus all the women. And when Rob emerged from the cab, she turned toward him with an amused smile.

Immediately, he correctly interpreted her reaction. "If you close your eyes and listen to the music, this explosion of red plush will fade to a mere pinkish glow behind your lids," he said, shutting off the lights. Once again they were plunged into a shadowy darkness, lit only by the stars glittering through the open skylight. The night had cooled down, and the breeze from the open windows and roof had now lowered the temperature in the van to a pleasant warmth.

"I think it will take more than music to rub out the red," she finally answered, a seductive note creeping into her voice.

"Let me see if I can be of assistance." He stepped forward and put his hands on her shoulders, drawing her against his lean, hard body. "You don't have to go back tonight, do you?"

"I should," she answered unconvincingly while she looked dreamily into his eyes.

"No, you shouldn't." Then his head lowered and his lips came down on hers. The kiss was both forceful and tender, and as Rob's mouth blended with hers, she knew that she would not be driving back to Washington that night. In the back of her mind she acknowledged that she was probably behaving unwisely again, but she couldn't help herself.

Lifting the hair from her neck, he stroked the sensitive flesh beneath with his fingertips, eliciting a sigh of pleasure from Pamela. His hands, tracing the delicate bone structure of her neck, moved against her skin while his moist lips tested the sweetness of her tongue with his own. Exciting sensations wavered across her slender shoulders as he rekindled the passion she'd felt for him earlier. But had it ever really left her? If she were honest with herself, she had to admit the truth. From the time he'd bounded into her life like a romantic ruffian from some fantasy epic, her desire for him had been simmering like hot brandy just before it reaches flame point. During the past month the only way to control that searing need had been to turn away from him. But tonight she wasn't willing to avoid the kindling heat of Rob's lustrous eyes, or of his kisses.

"We have the rest of the night, Pamela," he whispered, nuzzling the lobe of her ear. "Let's make this one we'll never forget."

"Oh, yes," she breathed. Life was too short not to accept what he offered her, she decided, even though she was unsure what would happen tomorrow. "Oh, yes," she repeated. "Let's have this night together."

Rob pulled her closer to his body so that she could feel him pressed hard against the firm flesh of her stomach. Slowly his hand traveled down her spine to the soft swell of her buttocks. Then, with maddening slowness, his hands slipped into the waistband of her jeans and she felt his fingers above the line of her panties. Her own hands moved to his broad back, feeling the firm muscles. But she wanted more. After tugging his shirt from his jeans, she ran her fingertips up and down the line of his backbone, reveling in the grace and power of his body.

"It's getting warm in here again," he said, moving his hands to the front of her jeans and unsnapping them. "I liked you better the way you were in the river."

The words brought her heated desires to a boil. "I liked you the way you were in the river, too," she answered in a breathy voice, as she unzipped his jeans.

"Oh, Pamela." He kissed her forcefully on the

mouth, before kneeling in front of her to peel the denim along with the wispy panties from her hips and thighs. When she stepped free of the restraining garments, he stroked his hand along the smooth curve of her belly and buried his face in its silky softness.

"I want you so much, it hurts." His voice had grown husky with emotion. "I've been wanting you for weeks. I kept sneaking glances at you all during the fair, but you never seemed to look my way."

Pamela smiled with secret pleasure at his admission. Sensuously she twined her long fingers in the thick hair curling around his ears. "Oh, no. I was looking at you, too."

"I hoped you were, but I couldn't tell. You seemed so damned remote," he whispered against her soft flesh. "I even tried to make you jealous, flirting with other women when I thought you might notice. But you didn't give me a glimmer of hope that you cared."

Bending over him, she kissed the top of his head and laced her fingers around the back of his neck. "I did," she murmured, "and I do. I was so jealous I wanted to throw a plateful of muffins at you."

He kissed her smooth skin again. Then standing, he looked at her with bedroom eyes. Taking her face in his hands, he said with a wink, "I wish you had tossed some of your goodies my way. I would have known what to do with them." Then his expression sobered, and lifting her chin, he asked, "Pamela, why have you tormented me this way, when you knew I wanted to be with you?"

Unable to answer, she drew his body to hers and held him close, her head resting on his shoulder. They stood that way for several minutes, drinking in the intoxicating nearness of each other. "Oh, Rob. It's all so confusing," she began, burying her face against his chest. "I guess I've been sorting out who I am." She searched for words. "I'm still not sure I recognize this Pamela Stewart. I'm just not the sort of woman who runs off and has affairs with dashing gypsy lovers."

"I'm not a gypsy," he corrected her. "I hold a steady job just like you."

This, she thought, pressing her breasts against him, wasn't the time for such a discussion. "You may not be a gypsy, but you've got dark mysterious eyes, a flashing smile and curls that would be the envy of any woman," she finally responded. "All you need is a dagger between your teeth and a gold earring in your ear."

Rob laughed and hugged her. "Ah ha! That sounds more like a pirate to me. And pirates are notorious for making off with beautiful women." With that, he scooped her up in his arms and kissed her until she was breathless. Then laying her down among the cushions on the van's plush floor, he unbuttoned her blouse so that her entire body was free for his marauding hands. "I think I like this pirate role," he announced. "This time I got a prize worthy of a king—a fine lady with tresses the color of warm toffee."

Pamela laughed with delight. What a wonderful way to describe hair that she considered an ordinary shade of brown.

But Rob's poetic praise was only just beginning. "With eyes of sunlit amber," he continued, running his fingers along the line of her eyebrow. Then he reached down and his lips softly brushed each eyelid. Lifting his head, he stroked her cheekbone and cupped her face between his palms. "I've said it before, and"—he grinned—"at the risk of being repetitious, I'll say it again. You're beautiful, Pamela Stewart."

Slowly, she shook her head, unable to accept his praise. "Oh, Rob. I'm not, but I love hearing you say it."

Rob curled a lock of her hair around his strong

fingers. "There you go again. Selling yourself short. Someday I must lecture you on that, but right now I'm going to finish cataloguing your assets."

Pamela had to grin. "You make me sound like a commodity."

"One I intend to invest in very shortly," he said, shifting his weight so that he could slide his hand down the hollow of her throat to her breasts. Tracing their full shape with his palm, he bent down, took one pink crest between his lips and teased it to a taut hardness.

Pamela moaned. Eagerly her hands went to the front of his shirt and fumbled with the buttons. "I want to touch you too," she murmured.

"Then we're in perfect accord," Rob said, sitting up and pulling off his shirt.

In the darkness, Pamela, admiring the outlines of his powerful shoulders, fanned her hands over the crisp hair that dusted his nipples and arrowed down to his flat belly. Suddenly he stood up, and not removing his eyes from her feminine curves, he tugged at his jeans.

Hungrily, she watched as he kicked away the garment and stood before her magnificantly naked. Once again, she admired the perfection of his male beauty. When she reached up imploringly, he obliged, lowering his body beside her on the soft carpet.

As her eyes followed his hands down the length of her slim figure, Pamela knew that this was a moment she would never forget. But soon the play of his touch on her body made even such thoughts as that impossible. She could do nothing but close her eyes and give herself up to the fiery sensations he was arousing.

"Oh, Rob," she gasped. Her fingers drew little circles along his back, feeling the steel beneath the velvet of his bronzed skin. Her rounded hips rose to meet his lean ones and she tried to draw him closer.

Responding to her burgeoning excitement, Rob

rolled over on top of her and kissed her deeply, his tongue plundering her sweetness. Pressed hard against her, his desire was obvious. And her own need was equally urgent.

Rob's hands had been clasped around her waist. Now they slipped down to her hips and raised them to meet his thrusting masculinity. When she felt him deep inside her, Pamela sighed at the perfection of the union. They seemed to fuse so beautifully.

Rob echoed her emotions. "Oh, Pamela, we belong together."

"Yes," she agreed as he began his rhythmic movements inside her. At first he was slow and deliberate. As she watched him arch over her, she saw above his head, through the skylight, a million points of light piercing the black heavens. The sexual tension building inside her made her think of comets on a collision course. Slowly, like brilliant galaxies, Pamela and Rob approached one another's superheated centers. And then they were coming together, exploding in a magnificent burst of light and heat. When the violent beauty of their union finally subsided, Rob collapsed against her, holding her tightly against his damp body.

He broke the ensuing silence first. "Pamela, under most circumstances, I'm a very verbal person. But for once, I'm at a loss for words."

"Don't talk then," she said tenderly. "Just hold me."

Rolling to one side, he clasped her length against him. For a few moments they lay there, savoring their closeness and watching the heavens.

Then Rob propped himself up on an elbow and grinned impishly at her. "If I were a true pirate, I'd make you walk the plank now."

Pamela put her hand to her breast and stared at him in mock indignation. "You mean after having your way with me, sir, you'd throw me to the sharks?"

He looked at her appraisingly. "Maybe I'd be a

reformed pirate, and I could make you my first mate. Then you could get up and swab the decks."

"Hmmph. You'd have to watch your step, then. I just might make the decks so soapy, you'd slide overboard and make a meal for the sharks yourself. Then I'd take over the ship."

Rob shook his head ruefully. "I'm afraid it's the sharks for you, then."

Pamela slapped playfully at him and giggled. "Maybe I'd better make my escape now that you're all tuckered out." She started to sit up and pretended to search for her clothes.

But Rob gently but firmly pushed her back down against the cushions. "This pirate doesn't let fair maidens escape so easily," he told her with a wicked grin. "If you spend the night with me, I won't make you swab the decks or walk the plank. I'll just kiss you unconscious."

Pamela nodded sagely. "Well, if I had to suffer a fate worse than death, that's the one I'd choose."

"Let's get started on it, then," he murmured, pulling her against him and kissing her soundly. Banging her fists ineffectually against his chest, she feigned a struggle, finally submitting to him with an unmartyrlike eagerness.

Several minutes later, Rob sat up against the cushions and raked a sinewy hand through his damp curls. "I don't know about you, but all this ravishing has made me thirsty. There's beer in the cooler. Would you like some?"

"Sounds good," Pamela agreed.

With easy grace, he sprang to his feet and climbed over the cushions on the floor. She heard the sounds of rummaging and then the snap of pop tabs being pulled. A moment later, unself-consciously naked, he returned and handed her a frosty can.

"Mmmm!" she exclaimed after taking a sip. "I'm not

all that fond of beer, but right now, this tastes delicious." She watched Rob's Adam's apple move as he downed the cool liquid.

While he swallowed, he nodded his agreement. "You know," he said when he finished, "I've worked this festival many times, but this year's fair has been very special."

"For me, too," she added, gazing at the chiseled outlines of his features. How many other women had he made love to like this? she wondered. But she wasn't going to ask, she scolded herself, banishing the disturbing question from her mind. Instead she began to query him about his career.

"What made you decide to become an actor?"

He leaned back into the cushions and took a sip of his beer. "That's a long story."

"I'm in the mood for one. Tell me a story, Dr. Robert Darcy." When the words were out of her mouth, she smiled. She'd never called him "Dr." before, but after all he was a PhD.

Rob chuckled. "It all started in high school. I was dating this girl who fancied herself a budding Sarah Bernhardt. Anyway she talked me into auditioning for a part in the school play. The drama coach had decided on *Romeo and Juliet,* and to my surprise, I ended up playing Romeo." He stopped and sipped contemplatively.

"How appropriate," Pamela exclaimed, thinking that Rob must have been the perfect star-crossed lover. With his curly hair, handsome face and exuberant manner, he would have bowled the high school girls over—just as he'd swept her off her feet. But, if she had known him in high school, she thought, remembering the skinny girl with braces that she'd been, she doubted Rob would have given her the time of day. She'd been so painfully shy, especially around boys. It was only during her first year of college that she'd gained some self-assurance, gotten rid of the braces and added the extra pounds that had so attractively filled out her frame. But even now, she wasn't exactly a social butterfly. A puzzled expression flitted over Pamela's face as she glanced up at his strong profile. She still found his apparent attraction to her mystifying, especially when he obviously could have any woman he wanted. Shifting her weight, she asked Rob another question.

"I know about stage-door Johnnies. Are there stage-door . . . Janes?" she ventured tentatively.

"Are you inquiring about my groupies?"

Pamela squirmed. "I guess I am."

Rob smiled and reached across to take her hand in his. "Pamela, I'm thirty-seven years old and you're certainly not the first woman I've kissed."

Kissed, Pamela assumed, was a euphemism for something much more intimate. And indeed, she fretted, it was obvious from Rob's expertise that he'd made love to many women. She'd known that all along and yet the thought stabbed her with a pang of jealousy. After all, he must have been intimate with sophisticated, beautiful women in the theatrical world. Suddenly Pamela found herself worrying about how she compared with such females.

Rob interrupted her by tenderly kissing her forehead. "Pamela, we're neither of us children and we've both been involved with other people, but what we've found together is very special—for me, at any rate," he added, looking at her questioningly through the dim light.

"Yes," she admitted. But her simple answer in no way indicated the depth of her feelings. For Pamela, their lovemaking had been a fantastic and liberating experience. Though in many ways she was still shy and self-conscious, she'd actually broken through the barrier of her inhibitions. Furthermore, she sensed that no matter what happened between her and Rob, she would never be quite the same person again.

"I know that you think of this Renaissance thing as some sort of interlude," Rob continued, his deep voice now very serious. "But I'd like it to be more than that between us."

Pamela's heart was beating like a hummingbird's wings as she waited to hear what he was going to say. The thought of ending this affair now was unbearable.

"I want to go on seeing you when we get back to Washington and the 'real' world," he said, dropping another kiss on her forehead. "Tell me you want the same thing."

"I do," Pamela found herself declaring without hesitation. "I want to go on seeing you, Rob." With those words, happiness welled up inside her. And as he set down the can of beer she was still holding, and took her in his arms, she went to him gladly.

8

As the sun shone through the skylight, its rays turned the interior of the van into a sea of glowing crimson and amethyst plush. The warm pinkish light made Pamela's eyelids flutter and then snap open wide. She nearly groaned as the flamboyant decor assaulted her senses. Last night this van had seemed vaguely exotic, like something out of *The Arabian Nights;* in daylight it looked like a punk rock star's bad trip.

Her gaze fell on the man sleeping next to her and traveled down the tanned length of his torso. He was sleeping like a baby, his head resting on one outstretched arm and his body curled up. Pamela shook her head and smiled at the relaxed expression on his face. Somehow the picture of him in this tawdry red lair was incongruous. How did he manage to sleep like a choirboy in such an inferno of color?

Propping herself up on the pillows, Pamela reached for her blouse and slipped it on. So much for being uninhibited, she thought, grinning at her own prudish reaction. She couldn't help but remember her feelings the last time she'd awakened with Rob beside her. Then she had gone tearing out of his apartment in a fit of embarrassment and guilt. While she didn't plan to behave so foolishly this time, now, in the bright morning light, she was feeling a bit self-conscious. Deliberately deciding to leave the blouse unbuttoned as a statement about the "new Pamela," she stretched out her long legs and considered the man next to her.

Last night had been a turning point in their relationship. Sighing, she remembered the touch of his long, sensitive fingers and the passion of his lovemaking. Despite the garish setting, it had been a memorable night, she thought, casting one more amused glance at the van's interior. And perhaps the most beautiful part had been Rob's last words to her. He'd said he wanted to continue seeing her. That wasn't exactly a declaration of love, but surely it represented some sort of commitment.

Turning her head, Pamela studied Rob's sleeping features. She could see some wisps of silver in his sideburns and the tracery of laugh lines around his eyes. He was no longer a teenaged Romeo, but he was still a devastatingly attractive man—one who'd lived an exciting and varied existence. Where did she fit in? Despite his many compliments the night before, in her heart Pamela couldn't believe that she was anywhere near his match. But perhaps if she stayed with him and accepted what he had to give her, some of his energy and enthusiasm for life would rub off on her.

Indeed, some already had, she acknowledged with a grin. This morning she felt very different from the Pamela Stewart who'd been so intimidated by Rob's dashing assault that first day of the Renaissance Festival. With an embarrassed shrug, she remembered how he'd rolled under her skirts, and she'd turned as red as the van's insides. The funny part was, here she was lying next to him now, not even wearing a skirt.

As she pondered this, Rob stirred and reached for her. Turning in her direction, he cupped his palm around her smooth elbow. "Mmmm," she heard him murmur groggily, "that feels good." He opened an eye and peered out at her. "But I'll bet with a little effort, I could find something that felt even better."

Pamela started to giggle as she felt his hand climb slowly up her arm. "You're impertinent, sir," she objected, brushing his exploring fingers away.

"One of my more endearing traits, don't you agree?" Rob retorted, sitting up and yawning. "I was afraid you might be gone, given past history. But you're still here. My only complaint is that you've got on too many clothes," he said, focusing on her unbuttoned blouse. "On the plus side, however, I like the way you're wearing them." He reached over and delicately stroked the curve of her breast.

"My one concession to modesty," Pamela said, enjoying the sensuous play of his hand on her soft skin. Just then her stomach gave an unromantic rumble and turned her mind to more practical concerns. "What are we going to do about breakfast?" she murmured. "There are still some muffins in my car."

Rob gave her a wicked grin and moved closer. "Your muffins are very fine, Pamela, my love. But I think I'd rather have you first."

Rolling over, he buried his lips in the valley between her warm breasts.

Sighing with pleasure at his touch, Pamela managed to say, "Now aren't you glad you didn't make me walk the plank last night?"

"Oh, very! There's something in this virtuous pirate business." Taking the tip of her nipple in his mouth, he suckled at it, and Pamela felt herself responding with all the fire of the previous night.

Suddenly a loud banging on the side of the van startled them from their loveplay. "Get up, Rob, you devil," a raucous female voice shouted. "It's almost nine, and you're wasting all this beautiful sunshine! Come on, up and at 'em!"

Rob groaned. "It's Tess. And once she starts, she never gives up. There'll be no ignoring her."

As though to confirm his observation, the clamor of her pep talk increased in volume. "I know you're in there, you rascal you! You'd better come out and give your old Tess a good-bye hug." She hit the side of the van once more and left the metal ringing so that Pamela felt as though she were sitting inside a clanging bell. "This is your last warning. I'm taking off for New York now, and I won't be seeing you for at least another year."

Exchanging a wry look with Pamela, Rob rose to his feet and ambled over to the window. Sticking his head out the small opening, he shouted enthusiastically, "Tess, my love, I wouldn't miss saying farewell for all the pirate gold in the world!" He shot Pamela a roguish wink and then turned back to the window.

"Pirate gold?" Tess exclaimed.

"Be right out!" Rob pulled the curtains shut and reached down to tug on his jeans. "Are you coming out to say good-bye to her?" he whispered to Pamela as he pulled a shirt over his head.

She stared up at him mutely. If she went out, it would be an open declaration that she and Rob were lovers and had spent the night together. Was she really up to that? No, she thought, shaking her head. She couldn't quite bring herself to go public yet. So much for the new Pamela. Maybe she wasn't such a changed woman after all.

Rob studied her for a moment, then squeezing her shoulder, he smiled and said, "I'll be back in a minute."

Pamela breathed a sigh of relief as she watched him

exit through the front of the cab. He was being considerate, careful not to expose her to view. Grateful for his understanding, she saw the doors close behind him. But while he was outside, the sound of his voice and Tess's drifted back into the van. As Pamela listened to their good-natured banter, she drew her knees up against her chest and hugged them. She would really like to be out there seeing off the kindly older woman who had befriended her. Putting a hand to her forehead, Pamela had to acknowledge that she felt ashamed of her inhibitions. After all, the people at the Renaissance Fair probably knew about her and Rob anyway. How silly it was to hide!

Scrambling to her feet, Pamela started gathering up her scattered clothes. She was just slipping into her sandals when the door of the van slid open and Rob came back in. "Tess just left. She sends her love."

The words made Pamela feel even worse. "I'm sorry I didn't have the nerve to go out there with you and say good-bye, but . . ." Her voice trailed off.

Rob squeezed her hand. "I understand. You're the bashful type. But you're going to have to get over that, my fair muffin maid. Because last night we decided that we were going to go on seeing each other—didn't we?" He gave her a questioning look.

Pamela looked at him, taking in his tousled black hair and broad naked chest. After last night, how could she say no? It might not be wise, but it was impossible to leave this man now. "Yes," she agreed once again, this time a little shyly.

Grinning from ear to ear, he took a step forward and swept her into his arms. "That's my Maid Muffin. Now we'll have to set out to make up for all the time lost during the festival!" He started to trail kisses along the tender skin of her neck while he stroked the small of her back.

Laughing at his audacity, Pamela tried to squirm out

of his embrace. "Stop that," she protested. "I'm afraid I'm not Maid Muffin anymore. You'll have to deal with plain old Pamela Stewart, and she," Pamela added, poking him playfully in the chest with her forefinger, "has to get back to work."

Rob pretended to look crushed. "Alas, so too must Robyn O'Dare. He must leave the merry glade and return to the prosaic concrete urban jungle of Washington, D.C.

Pamela made a face. Privately, she thought, there was nothing prosaic about her lover's job. His real life was almost as romantic as the fantasy one he had created for the festival. Whereas she, on the other hand, would be going back to a desk full of papers, statistics, budgets and memos. But there would be one important difference, she admitted, running a finger along Rob's broad shoulder. For the next few weeks, at least, there was going to be a man named Robert Darcy in her life—and in her bed.

The days that followed were a blur of color and activity in Pamela's mind. The sabbatical had refreshed her and given her a new outlook so that now her hours in the office appeared full of challenging opportunities, a fact that she'd lost sight of in the past. Feeling more creative, she found herself enthusiastically participating in the process of brainstorming new programs and developing ideas. The fall season had brought in a fresh batch of innovative proposals, ones that stimulated her with their unique possibilities, and she plunged into the review process with vigor.

During the following days, Gunther, her boss, took note of her renewed excitement about her work. One morning, two weeks after her return, he leaned over her desk and exclaimed, "Pamela, selling muffins must be a real tonic."

She eyed him curiously. "What do you mean?" she

asked, but she already knew what he was referring to. It was almost as if she wanted her own perceptions confirmed.

And Gunther did that with his next statement. "Not only are you looking brighter these days, you seem to have more vitality, more ideas. Maybe," he added, his bulky frame shaking with a jolly laugh, "I should put on some green tights and sell a few muffins myself next summer."

Pamela was amused by the absurd image of her rotund boss in tights, but the young grants administrator was also pleased with his words.

What was more, Gunther's observation was confirmed by her friend Sheilah. At lunch later that week the pert blond corporate lawyer sat with her shapely legs crossed, studying Pamela and nodding her head. "I guess I have to admit it. I was wrong when I told you that you were crazy to go sell rum cakes at a Renaissance festival. Ever since your vacation you've been like a different woman. I can't wait to meet this guy, Rob," she added, leaning over the table and tapping her friend on the arm. "He must really be something."

"Maybe I'll introduce you sometime soon," Pamela hedged. She wasn't ready to share Rob with anyone else yet. It was as if she'd found the key to a treasure, and she feared that if she revealed the secret, the precious find would vanish in a puff of smoke. There'd be time enough to show Rob off later, Pamela told herself, knowing full well her possessive feelings about him were a bit irrational.

"Everything about you is brighter," Sheilah remarked as she picked at her seafood salad. "Especially your eyes. Is it your love life, or have you gotten those contact lenses that enhance your eye color?"

Pamela started to laugh. That remark was typical of Sheilah's humor. "No," she assured the lawyer, "it's not contacts. It's happiness."

Ever since their tryst in that ridiculous van, she and Rob had either talked by phone each day or seen each other. Sometimes they'd meet for an impromptu picnic lunch on the grass by the Tidal Basin. Other times, they'd plan an elaborate evening. Rob was an inveterate experimenter and was teaching her to be one as well. He had made it a point to dine at different ethnic restaurants, trying out everything from Ethiopian food to fancy French cuisine.

But more often they ate at either her place or Rob's. She loved cooking all her specialities for him, especially nouvelle cuisine dishes—a light version of French. Rob, as it turned out, was an excellent chef himself. Meals at his house generally consisted of spicy Szechuan fare that he stirred up in a large wok. And after each of these elegant candlelit dinners full of laughter and intimate conversation, they always wound up making sweet, passionate love.

Every time Pamela found herself waiting for Rob's knock on the door, she felt like a wide-eyed child with a fistful of tickets in an amusement park. It was like being a little girl who captured the brass ring on the merry-go-round—not just once but everytime her high flying steed took her past the glittering prize. And like that child, she never wanted the ride to end.

But the practical side of Pamela kept whispering, "This can't last. Nothing this good ever does." For three weeks, she'd managed to muffle that little voice. But deep inside she feared the day that the tickets would run out and the glittering prize would elude her grasping fingers. And sure enough, one night the carousel ground to a shuddering halt.

Almost all of Pamela's time with Rob had been spent alone with him, except for one double date with Jake and his girlfriend Carolyn. They'd embarked on a rollicking trip to a crab house on the Chesapeake Bay where they'd wielded wooden mallets to crack open dozens of blue crabs spread out on a brown-paper-covered table. Other than that one expedition, she and Rob had kept to themselves.

Reality intruded on their romantic twosome when Rob invited her to a party given by one of his theater friends.

"What should I wear?" she asked him, anxious that she make the right impression on his friends.

But Rob only laughed at the apprehensive expression on her face and kissed the tip of her nose. "Wear anything you like," he told her with a careless wave of his hand. "At these parties anything goes, and I know that whatever you wear, you'll look beautiful."

"Thanks a heap," she answered, feeling a bit at sea. "You're a big help."

"We aim to please," he replied, pulling her down on the couch next to him and silencing her with a very thorough kiss.

But when the night of the party arrived, Pamela stood in front of her closet stewing over its contents. Her eyes roamed over the row of business suits and conservative work dresses. She frowned. Nothing seemed right. She would have gone out and purchased something special, but she'd been busy and Rob had been so vague that she'd been lulled into a false sense of security. She raised a critical eyebrow at a navy dress she'd taken out and then stuffed the rejected garment back, wishing once more that she'd pinned Rob down.

After mentally sorting through her wardrobe for the tenth time, she finally pulled out an old standby, a simple but well-cut blue silk dress. Though there was nothing unusual about the garment, its conservative lines made it a good all-purpose dress for almost any occasion short of a backyard barbeque or a reception for Queen Elizabeth at Buckingham Palace.

Later, when she opened the front door, Rob stood in front of her wearing dark slacks and an open-collared cream silk shirt. He looked dashing in an elegantly simple way. "Maybe I ought to change," were the first words out of her mouth.

"That's a fine greeting." He gave her a kiss and then looked her up and down. "You look sensational."

"Do you think I'm overdressed? I just have no idea what everyone will be wearing."

Rob drew her out the door. "What are you so nervous about? You act as if we're going to a formal state dinner at the White House. Believe me, these are just some of my old theater buddies—they're just people like you and me."

Pamela's eyes widened, but she held her tongue. Maybe they're just like him, she thought as he showed her into his Volvo, but they're certainly not going to be like me.

And they certainly weren't, she noted as they stood at the front door of the beautiful Georgetown townhouse where the party was being held. The renovated brick building belonged to well-known artist Reed Prestwood, who had done set designing for the theater. Obviously, he'd done quite well for himself, she thought as she admired the stately three-story facade. Its grande dame appearance suggested elegant tea parties and sumptuous balls with women in long gowns.

But immediately after the massive wooden door swung open, she was hit by the sounds of loud laughter and frenetic conversation. "Come in and welcome," greeted their host, a slightly tipsy man with shoulder-length curls. "Drinks are over to the right, and food," he added, airily motioning with a cigarette in a silver holder, "is just behind that glorious redhead with the obvious panty-lines marring her otherwise perfect posterior."

Glancing over their host's shoulder, Pamela spotted the young lady in question, a gorgeous creature with a

flaming mane, decked out in clinging white silk pajamas
and a silver lamé tee-shirt. Panty-lines or no, she made
Pamela feel dowdy.

Playing nervously with her pearl necklace, Pamela
distracted herself by studying the unusual design of the
house. They were standing in an entry high above the
main floor and while Rob chatted with Reed, she
peered down into the living room. With its dramatic
cathedral ceilings, expanses of glass and multilevel
design, the house reminded Pamela of a stage set for a
modernistic drama. Though the exterior was fashion-
ably old, the furnishings and decor inside were startlingly contemporary, even futuristic—quite a contrast to
Pamela's more traditional taste. Suddenly, her eye was
drawn to several huge canvases splashed with bold
squiggles of color.

"Those are some paintings done by Reed a few years
ago for an exhibition at the Hirshorn," Rob said,
breaking away from his distracted host and gesturing at
what looked to Pamela like the creations of an industrious kindergartener with a box of oil paints.

"Oh," she said, unsure what the proper reaction to
the colorful but bewildering paintings was. "Interesting," she finally commented, wondering, but afraid to
ask, what Rob thought of his friend's art. They'd
covered all manner of subjects in their many talks, but
they'd never really gotten around to discussing their
tastes in art. Could it be that Rob really liked this sort of
thing? She thought that living with a painting like the
hideous orange and red piece to her right would give
her a perpetual migraine headache.

As Rob led her down the stairs, her gaze traveled
around to the people massed in the spacious living
room. The first thing that hit her was the getups they
wore wearing. Rob had said that "anything goes" at
these parties, and he hadn't been exaggerating. Some
of the guests lounged about in torn tee-shirts, safety pin

earrings and punk rock hair dyed purple and green. Others dressed in what looked like Reed's paintings transformed into clothing—bold grafitti prints and foot-high teased hair. And then there were the women in flamboyant confections of feathers and shiny beads, their faces painted with a rainbow of makeup colors. Some of the men were dressed more simply, like Rob. But only a handful of the women were, she noted ruefully. Pamela looked down at her plain blue dress. She felt like a little brown sparrow at a convention of birds of paradise.

Immediately, she wondered where the bathroom was. Maybe she could hide in it all night. How long did Rob want to stay in this place? she asked herself. Was there any chance that they could just put in an appearance and leave? She had only to glance over at him for the answer. Smiling broadly as he led her through the gaudy group, he looked not only at ease, but as if he anticipated an interesting evening. Though he wasn't sporting glitter or violet hair like many of the others, his dark good looks and simple clothing made him stand out like a sleek black panther in a cage full of spotted and striped felines. On the other hand, if she was noticeable, she was sure it was as the drabbest female in the room.

As these thoughts ran through Pamela's head, she glanced around, almost in panic, at the swirling activity. How would she ever manage to get through an evening in this exotic environment? What would she have to say to these people? The snatches of conversation that she overheard were bewildering.

"My costume for that one"—Pamela caught one woman exclaiming—"was nothing but a glorified g-string."

"He's taken up with another man and now they have a ménage à trois," confided another in a startlingly loud voice.

Nonplussed, Pamela followed Rob as he wound his way toward the bar, stopping every few feet to exchange greetings with old acquaintances. She hung back self-consciously. "Hello," was the brightest remark she could muster as he introduced her.

Just as Rob was handing Pamela a glass of champagne, a woman draped in a kimono and painted in heavy white geisha makeup rushed up to him and threw her arms around his neck. For a long moment they swayed together in a hug. "Rob, you old devil, where have you been?" the remarkable-looking woman exclaimed as she pulled back to admire the actor. "Natasha has been absolutely morose since you abandoned her."

Pamela's jaw dropped. Who was Natasha?

But she couldn't linger on that problem for long, because Rob was drawing her up to the kimono-wrapped woman and introducing her. "Pamela, this is Jaimie De Vere, an old road show pal. Jaimie, this is Pamela Stewart, a grants administrator at the Harley Rutherford Foundation."

Before Pamela could get out an "I'm pleased to meet you," the geisha leaned forward and tapped the young woman's wrist with her fan. "So, you administer grants. Hmmmm." She eyed Pamela speculatively, taking in her conservative attire. "Do you have any extra money lying about? You know, a few thou here or there? I could sure use it. We artistic types," she said, casting a conspiratorial look at Rob and nudging him with her hip, "are always broke."

Smiling a bit thinly, Pamela shook her head. "I'm afraid the funding for this past fiscal year is all used up. If you want to apply for next year . . ." But Jaimie had already turned away to finish her conversation with Rob, and Pamela's voice trailed off as she realized no one was listening.

For several minutes the other two reminisced while

Pamela stood shifting her weight from one foot to the other. Already the high-heeled sandals she was wearing were beginning to chafe. Needing something to do while the two of them talked, Pamela looked down into her drink and swirled the ice. Even though Rob was trying to include her in the conversation, she felt like an eavesdropper.

Finally, when it seemed as though Rob and the geisha had exhausted their reminiscences, Jaimie turned toward Pamela once again. "My dear, you look like the innocent type," the actress said, giving Rob a teasing sideways look, "so I'd better warn you about this man. Don't you believe his silver tongue. He's really quite a rogue," she continued, swatting at him playfully with her fan. "He broke my poor heart ten years ago and I still bear the scars." She thumped her chest and struck a mournful pose.

Rob let out a crack of laughter and the woman smiled. "Jaimie, your heart is made up of old playbills. The only thing that breaks it is bad reviews and less than star billing."

"Touché," she said, giving him a hug. Then winking broadly, she turned to a bewildered Pamela. "Well, I must go circulate. If this rake doesn't take good care of you, let me know." With another little flourish of her fan, she drifted away.

"Where do you know her from?" Pamela demanded in what she hoped was a light tone. Jaimie's remark had disturbed her more than she was willing to show. People always seemed to be warning her about Rob's roguish ways. Maybe she should start listening for a change.

"Jaimie and I go way back." Rob grinned as he answered Pamela's query. "We started out in summer stock together and occasionally our paths still cross. She's quite a character, don't you think?"

"Yes," Pamela agreed sincerely. "But I'm not sure I

liked her warning. You do have quite a reputation, don't you, Robert Darcy?"

But he only chuckled. "Oh, Jaimie's a comedienne—a great kidder. Don't believe anything she says." Then an old friend caught Rob's eye and he raised a palm in greeting. Grabbing Pamela's hand, he began once more to lead her through the crowd. "There are some people I want you to meet," he told her over his shoulder.

A moment later he had introduced her to a group of actors and actresses that he'd worked with in a repertory company during his college vacations. In a moment, they and Rob had launched into tales about their youthful hijinks. Each anecdote, Pamela noted, was punctuated by gales of laughter. The stories, particularly the one about the pompous old actor who'd patronized them outrageously during one play's run, amused her too. According to Rob, at the last performance, the company had teamed up to put a dead mouse in a cup that the conceited player was supposed to gaze lovingly into while delivering a profound soliloquy.

As the group chatted, their camaraderie and shared experience made Pamela sad. She realized all too clearly how much her background differed from Rob's. These people were verbal acrobats, quick with puns and other word play. Like Rob, they shared a free and easy attitude toward life. If only she could talk half as cleverly, and be half as unfettered, she thought.

Now the conversation turned to tidbits about old acquaintances, so Pamela couldn't even pretend to join in their discussion. Feeling phony because she was smiling at things she didn't even understand, Pamela was relieved to see Jake coming toward them. He appeared to be alone.

"Where's Carolyn?" Pamela asked when he came up alongside her.

"En route to Paris where she's clinching a deal with a cosmetics company."

Pamela's eyebrows shot up. "Paris," she sighed. "That's one impressive lady you've got."

"You can say that again. I only wish I were touring Gay Paree together with her," Jake answered, taking a sip of Scotch.

"I wish I were too," Pamela whispered close to her friend's ear. "I feel like a fish out of water in this crowd."

Jake looked up at the group Pamela had inched away from. "Oh, they're quite a lively crew, those guys."

"They make my head swim."

Jake patted her on the shoulder. "Give them a chance. They're great people once you get to know them."

"Oh, I think they're wonderful. It's just that I can't keep up. They talk faster than I think."

Glancing back, Pamela saw that the group had just broken up and that Rob had been swept into the center of another bevy of actors. Smiling, he caught her eye, waved at her and Jake. Obviously deciding that she was taken care of, he leaned down to listen to a short woman who was animatedly telling a story. Apparently, what she had to say amused him, for in a moment, they were both roaring.

Turning to her friend, Pamela realized that Jake had been studying the expression on her face. Quickly, she rearranged her frown into a smile.

"Parties like this are tough on newcomers, but if you stay with Rob, you'll get the hang of it," he assured her.

"Maybe I'll try that," she said, attempting to sound sure of her words. But privately, she was beginning to wonder if she would be up to attempting the struggle.

As she pondered this, a robust silver-haired man, dressed in jeans and a tee-shirt, latched onto Jake and began jabbering a mile a minute. He turned out to be a playwright who wanted Jake's opinion on his latest project. Though the former jester tried hard to include Pamela in their discussion, she could tell it was a strain.

Finally, she patted her diminutive protector on the shoulder and whispered, "I'm going to go look for Rob." Then turning to the garrulous writer, she added, "Nice meeting you."

He nodded but continued to talk a blue streak, and Pamela walked away. As she wandered through the milling group, she didn't spot Rob right away and she began to feel anxious and very alone. Everywhere she looked strangers happily conversed, lost in each other's company. She couldn't picture herself breaking into any of these tight-knit groups and introducing herself. What would she say to them? Give some hints on baking rum cakes? Offer them grants if they'd be nice to her?

After a few minutes of standing by herself, she felt even more conspicuous. Her feet really hurt her now, and her head had started to throb from the noise, smoke and tension.

Finally, through the tangle of people, Pamela saw Rob in the midst of another spirited group. He was making strange motions with his hands. Stopping, she put one hand on her hip and squinted. They appeared to be playing a game of some type. Charades, she realized, watching Rob mimic driving a car. She hated charades. But Rob was obviously in his element. His black eyes sparkled with merriment; and as his hand limned a new element of the message he was trying to convey, his whole body seemed alive with the challenge of the game.

Fearing that he might notice her and draw her into the activity, Pamela took a step back. The few times she'd played charades, she'd frozen up and no one had managed to guess her message. Maybe this was the appropriate time to find the bathroom, she decided. Probably by now her makeup needed refreshing anyhow.

It took her several minutes to locate a powder room and when she found it, it was occupied. After putting her glass down on a nearby end table, she took a place in line behind the two women before her. As she waited she couldn't help but notice their flamboyant clothing. One wore a beaded Indian headband, skin-tight jeans and a small fringed vest with no blouse beneath it. The other, a striking blonde in a white satin dress trimmed with maribou, seemed straight out of a thirties musical. Pamela was just studying the fluffy white feathers and wishing she could touch them when she heard one of the pair mention Rob's name. Instinctively, Pamela stiffened.

"That Rob Darcy. He's still a foxy guy. I had the biggest crush on him when we did *Streetcar* together," confided the bogus Indian maiden. "But," she sighed, "he had the hots for Marilyn Tarcher at the time."

"Oh, yeah. That cute little brunette with the big blue eyes. Who's he got on the string now?" the other asked.

"Oh, he's a clever old fox. He's got himself fixed up with a grants administrator from some big foundation, I hear."

"Oh," the blonde cooed. "Good old Rob, I guess he won't have to worry about getting his grant next year. I certainly would be happy to grant him anything," she added in a sultry May West voice.

"Me, too," the "Indian" agreed as the bathroom door opened and she disappeared into it.

Now, in addition to her throbbing head and aching feet, a sickening sensation had arisen in Pamela's stomach. All evening she'd felt out of place, but now the anxiety that had been simmering for hours erupted. Pamela knew Rob wasn't seeing her because of her position with the foundation, but the innuendo was disturbing. It wasn't surprising, she realized, that other people thought that. After all, they probably looked at her and wondered what she had that would attract a charismatic man like Robert Darcy. Pamela still wondered about that, too.

Looking around at the flashy crowd of chattering theater people, she acknowledged that Rob belonged in this setting. She didn't. The past few weeks she'd been living in a fool's paradise. All of a sudden she felt like she'd been staring in a fun house mirror for hours. She had to get out of this place right now. She didn't belong here with these human peacocks.

Turning away abruptly, Pamela began to search for her escort once again. Before long she spotted him, still in the center of a crowd of charade players. She saw him scan the crowd for a moment and realized that he was probably wondering where she'd gotten to. Catching sight of her, he smiled, a look of relief flickering in his eyes before he turned back to his friends.

As she moved toward him Pamela frantically tried to invent plausible excuses for leaving. Maybe she could tell him she had a headache. Her temples really were pounding.

When she got within a few feet of the group, she paused to study him. His animated face told her that he was enjoying the spotlight and in no mood to leave. She would be spoiling his fun. I'll just tell him that I'll take a taxi, she thought, stepping forward once again.

But when she approached the circle of people surrounding him, she realized that he was in the middle of telling another funny story. The others were looking up at him expectantly, their eyes glimmering as they watched his expressive hands parody a well-known Shakespearean character actor who'd stopped off overlong at a bar before a performance of *Hamlet*. Shifting from one blistering foot to the other, Pamela waited for her lover to finish the narrative. But he no sooner concluded that one, than he began another and then another.

Finally, no longer able to restrain her impatience, Pamela went to him and touched his elbow. "Rob," she ventured quietly, "can I talk to you?"

Stopping mid-phrase he gave her an irritated look. She'd obviously broken his timing. "In a minute," he replied, dismissing her and quickly turning back to his eager audience.

For Pamela, that was the last straw. Any other woman might judge her behavior as irrational, but Pamela's head hurt, her feet ached and an overwhelming depression had engulfed her. She felt like an airsick space traveler on an alien planet. Without waiting for Rob to finish, she headed for the door.

Just before she reached it, she bumped into a concerned-looking Jake. "What's wrong?" he asked, looking into her reddened eyes. "You look like you've just found a cockroach swimming the backstroke in your punch."

Despite her churning emotions, a ghost of a smile curved her pale lips. "You're close."

"Let's see," he said, putting a finger to his lip. "The hors d'oeuvres are too salty—bad for the heart." She shook her head. "Some insidious soul watered down your drink."

"No, Jake, it's nothing . . . this just isn't my kind of party." She gestured around them. "And I don't feel well. Look," she said, putting a hand on her friend's shoulder, "maybe you could do me a favor. Rob's busy with his friends and I haven't been able to get to him. Please tell him I have a headache and had to go." Quickly, hoping to escape Jake's further questions, she pushed her way through the door, but he followed her.

"Let me take you home. Taxis are hard to find this time of night."

"Oh, Jake. You don't have to."

"Yes, I do," he insisted, taking her arm and leading her down the block to where his car was parked.

Pamela smiled warmly at him. "Jake," she said, linking her arm with his, "you're a real friend."

It was several minutes before Rob finished his storytelling. While his friends chuckled appreciatively, he looked around and noticed that Pamela wasn't there anymore. Where had she gone to? he asked himself, moving toward the bar to refresh his drink. As he eyed the dazzling array of half-empty bottles, a few more friends came up to chat and another half hour passed before he could pull away and continue his search. He was feeling guilty for leaving her on her own, but, he reasoned, it was probably good for her. Maybe she'd realize that she could handle this group, or any other for that matter. Taking a sip of his Scotch, he recalled her lack of self-assurance about what to wear and what to say to his friends. He shook his head. It didn't make any sense. She was a beautiful, successful, intelligent woman. Yet, she continued to think of herself as some sort of wallflower, a shrinking violet among vibrant tiger lilies.

But perhaps it was that very quality of modesty that had attracted him, he thought as he looked for her golden brown mane among the crowd. He'd always spent his time with theatrical types like himself. Now, after knowing Pamela, he realized that the women he was accustomed to seemed brittle and contrived. Pamela's naturalness was refreshing, and he knew he'd never settle for anything less again.

As he scanned the faces around him he frowned slightly. Where was she? The answer was provided moments later by Jaimie, who pranced up to him and placed her arm around his shoulder. "Looking for someone?" she said coyly.

"Yes, I seem to have lost Pamela. Have you seen her?"

"Oh," she answered. "Yes, I have. I don't think your lady friend's too fond of us." The actress paused and waved her fan. "Your date left arm and arm with Jake an hour or so ago. I just happened to have run out to get something from my car and I saw them walk off." She gave Rob an arch look. "Guess that means you're on your own."

"Not for long," Rob said grimly, taking a swig of his drink. Then, setting his glass on the bar, he turned and headed for the door.

9

━━━∞∞∞∞∞∞∞∞∞∞━━━

As Pamela settled back into the gray velour seat of Jake's car she stared out the window at the passing streets of Georgetown. It was a Friday night and people clad in bizarre outfits spilled out from trendy bars and cafés into the streets. Certainly there were normal-looking couples, men in suits and women in dresses, and some casually dressed in blue jeans. However, punk rockers and other "individualists" vied for side-walk space.

As Pamela eyed a young woman with glitter-dusted Day-Glo hair, another jab of pain hit her throbbing temple. She was beginning to feel that it wasn't just a case of not fitting in with Rob's friends, but that she didn't fit in anywhere. It seemed as if the whole world had turned into a parade of comic book characters and she was playing straight man—or woman. The observation did nothing to lighten her distressed mood, and she sighed heavily.

"Want to tell your old buddy Jake what this is all about?" the sympathetic man next to her inquired.

Pamela sighed again. "I'd like to get home and swallow a couple of aspirin first."

"Can I take that as an invitation to come in and talk?"

She hadn't really thought of her comment as an invitation, but maybe it wasn't such a bad idea. She'd really been keeping everything in, and besides, she didn't want to be alone right then. "Of course," she agreed.

A few minutes later she was showing Jake into her townhouse. "Nice place you have here. It looks like you," he said, glancing around at the mix of antiques and country furnishings.

"Make yourself comfortable," she replied over her shoulder as she headed toward the bathroom medicine cabinet. "I'll be right with you."

After Pamela had downed some aspirin, she offered to make a pot of coffee. Jake accepted and followed her into the plant-filled kitchen with its pressed oak furniture and ceramic tile counters. Ducking under a low-hanging fern, he positioned himself behind a chair and rested his hands on its back. Neither spoke while Pamela pulled out the coffee can and busied herself with the preparations.

"Well?" Jake finally said as he watched his hostess measure the coffee into the basket.

Pamela stopped with a scoop of ground coffee poised over the pot. "Well," she repeated in a slightly shaky voice, "I guess I'm just not the dramatic type. I don't fit into Rob's crowd."

Jake tilted his head and gave her an amused, questioning look. "Walking out the way you did seems rather dramatic to me, don't you think?" Then his expression sobered. "What's wrong, Pamela?"

She was quiet as she plugged in the coffeemaker. Then taking a deep breath, she turned toward her guest and proclaimed, "I think I've been kidding myself for the past few weeks." She nervously fingered a fold in her dress. "Almost any woman would be swept off her feet by a man like Rob, but I just don't think I'm showy or clever enough to keep up with him. After tonight, I'm sure I could never be comfortable with his friends. And we certainly can't maintain a relationship in isolation. I mean"—she gestured helplessly as she sank down into a kitchen chair—"we can't cut ourselves off from the rest of the world indefinitely."

Jake cocked his head. "I'm a friend of Rob's."

"I know and you once warned me about him yourself. Remember?"

For a moment Jake looked stunned. Then a frown creased his brow. "Surely, you're not talking about what I said after Rob crushed your rum cakes?" When he saw the expression on her face, he drew back. "Oh, Pamela," he declared, shaking his head with concern, "I never meant that to be taken seriously. It was just part of the act—dramatic license. Like Rob, I was just playing a role."

But she wasn't convinced. "Maybe, but you're not always on stage the way Rob and his friends seem to be."

Jake laughed at that. "That doesn't sound like me at all. I'm forever being accused of hamminess." He pulled out the seat opposite Pamela, sat down and leaned toward her. "Listen, parties like that affect a lot of people strangely. First of all," he said, "these gatherings aren't purely social. They're business. There's a lot of making contacts and jockeying for parts going on. People come to a bash like that to be noticed and remembered." He gave her a searching look. "You're a high level professional; don't you have this sort of thing going on in your world, too?"

Pamela had to admit she did. Cocktail parties that were really work sessions were common enough. But on those occasions no one came dressed in clownish makeup, and the atmosphere was quite different—high powered, yet sedate.

"But, Jake . . ." she began to protest.

He cut her off. "Now, really Pamela," he started, taking her hand and giving it a friendly squeeze. "Don't you think you might be overreacting a bit? After all, you've got to take these things for what they are. Don't let a bad party ruin a good relationship."

Pamela got up to pour the coffee. "Maybe I'm not being sensible about this evening, but it showed me something," she persisted. "Rob and I live in different worlds. We're all right together when it's just the two of us. But sooner or later, like tonight, the outside intrudes." She got up and poured the coffee into mugs. "You know, what really upsets me most," she added, offering her friend a mug, "is that all the time I've been with him, I've had the feeling that I was an imposter."

Jake accepted the coffee mug and sipped thoughtfully. "I think what's really bothering you is that Rob was 'on' tonight. But Pamela, remember, the guy's an actor. Sometimes he falls into a role. It doesn't mean it's a real person you're seeing."

"But how do I know when he's real?" she demanded. "Maybe our relationship is all an act. Maybe he'll get tired of the part."

"Pamela . . ." Jake began, looking slightly exasperated. A loud pounding on the front door broke into their conversation. They shot one another a long look, each knowing that it must be Rob.

Flustered, Pamela sprang to her feet and knocked over her coffee. "Oh," she muttered in frustration.

"Here, you get the door. I'll take care of the mess," suggested Jake, waving her on. As he spoke, he strode to the counter and pulled a few paper towels off the roll hanging below the cabinets.

Pamela had started out to the foyer, when she

suddenly turned and looked back into the kitchen. "What will I say to him?" she asked, a note of panic in her voice.

Jake was bending over the table swabbing up the puddle of dark liquid that was threatening to drip down the wooden pedestal and spread onto the floor. He looked up. "Just tell him the truth. It's better to get your feelings out in the open."

"I suppose so," Pamela said, sounding unconvinced as she turned on her heel and walked resignedly to the front door, much like a prisoner facing a firing squad.

The expression on Rob's face when she got there didn't suggest that he would hear her sympathetically. He was scowling, his dark eyebrows pulled together in an angry line. His mouth had a grim cast, and the stiff way he held his hands on his hips suggested that the next few minutes would be stormy ones. "Walking out on me seems to be a habit of yours," he thundered as he strode past her to the lighted kitchen. Narrowing her eyes, Pamela shut the door and followed behind him.

Jake was just taking a final swipe at the floor as Rob's tall frame filled the doorway. "Great! My best friend." He shook his head as his eyes went from Pamela to Jake. "Just what the hell are you doing here?" Without giving the other man a chance to reply, Rob shot Pamela an accusing look. "Not only do you run off without saying a word, but you do it with a guy I thought was my buddy."

"Wait a minute, Rob," Jake protested, straightening up and raising a hand. "This is not what you think."

Rob's eyes were slits. "Oh, and what am I supposed to think?" It was more a statement than a question.

The smaller man began another explanation, but Pamela stopped him. "I'd like to handle this, Jake," she ventured boldly.

"Yes," Rob drawled sarcastically. "Go on home and let the lady handle the situation."

"Are you sure, Pamela?" Jake asked.

Pamela nodded.

"Okay. As long as you think you're going to be all right." Obviously quite willing to make his escape, Jake placed the wet towel on the counter, touched Pamela on the shoulder and walked out, closing the door quietly behind him.

When he was gone, she and Rob eyed each other warily.

"You don't really think I was with Jake because there's something between us, do you?"

Rob studied her guardedly. "No," he finally admitted to her as well as to himself. "But I'd still like an explanation of why you stood me up at the party in front of all my friends and left with him."

"It was because of those friends of yours," she snapped. "They weren't interested in holding a civilized conversation. All they wanted to do was strut around in their fine feathers and crow about their triumphs."

Once more a scowl darkened Rob's features. "That's unfair."

Pamela bit her lip. She knew she was exaggerating, but she'd found the whole scene so distasteful that she wasn't about to back down now. Taking a step forward, she put her hands on her hips and challenged him once more. "Your friends gave me a headache," she retorted.

"My friends gave you a headache!" He folded his arms across his chest in a belligerent attitude. "Well, at least I have friends! Either you're too ashamed to introduce me to yours or you don't really have any."

Rob's words stung her. There was an element of truth in what he said. She didn't have lots of friends like Rob did. Her friends were special, and the truth was that she had deliberately not introduced them to him. She hadn't been ready to share him.

But that was not the explanation she offered Rob.

"My friends would probably bore a man of the world like you," she blurted out unjustly. "They don't go around wearing geisha getups or Indian headbands and none of them have purple hair!"

Rob nodded and began to pace back and forth in front of her. "You're a real snob. Do you know that?"

Pamela was shocked and insulted. "Snob! Just what do you mean by that crack?"

"Just what I said. You turned up your nose at my friends. You didn't even make an effort to talk to them. You had them pegged before you met them."

Pamela turned white with indignation. "That isn't true," she flared. "They didn't want to talk to me. And frankly," she added, her brown eyes taking on a fiery glint, "I didn't know what to say to them. What do you say to a guy dressed in five tons of gold chains and a Mohawk haircut?"

"Wait a minute," Rob protested. "Don't mistake everyone who dropped in at Reed's for one of my friends."

But Pamela, her anger building, pressed on. "And why didn't you warn me to wear something that wouldn't make me stand out like a sore thumb?" she rasped, staring down at the severe lines of her simple dress. "I felt like Alice in Wonderland at the Mad Hatter's tea party."

For a moment Rob looked baffled. "You looked just fine."

"I did not look fine," she almost shouted. "All of your pals were staring at me and wondering what you were doing with—" she searched for an image—"Little Miss Muffet."

Rob looked amused. "How about 'Little Miss Muffin'?"

Pamela didn't laugh; she was too worked up. "It's no joking matter. We're great together in bed, but there's more to a relationship than sex."

Rob threw up his hands in exasperation and turned his back on her. "Haven't I heard this song and dance before? Don't you ever get tired of it?" He turned back and gave her a piercing look. "We've already been through this at least a thousand times, Pamela. I'm sick of it."

"So, okay, you're sick of it, but we always skirt around it. Maybe you're the love 'em and leave 'em type, but I'm not." She thumped her chest and glared at him.

His eyes blazed with anger at her remark. But before he could answer her charge, she added, "I'm not one for flings. Anyhow"—her voice had grown softer now, —"the more I get involved with you, the more frightened I become."

There it was, Pamela suddenly realized—her deepest fear had surfaced. From the beginning of her love affair with Rob, she'd been afraid that it was nothing more than a summertime interlude for him, a mere temporary diversion. And though she wanted to believe him and told herself time and again that he loved her, she knew she really couldn't believe that it was true.

Rob's dark eyes flashed. "You're just handing out insults right and left tonight, aren't you? Next thing you know, you'll be calling me a gigolo and accusing me of being after one of your grants."

Pamela turned red. "No," she answered truthfully, but she was embarrassed because she'd considered it.

When he saw her equivocal expression, Rob's jaw dropped. "My God! I've hit the nail on the head."

"No," she tried to explain, but his deep baritone drowned her out.

"You really do think some garbage like that." He glared at her. "I had no idea you had such a low opinion of me—as well as of yourself."

"Myself?"

"Yes, all that 'poor little me' stuff you've been dishing

out. 'I'm too dull, too boring . . .'" he said in a high whining voice that put her teeth on edge. "Well, let me set you straight on some points. First of all, I am not some cheap Lothario. I've known a few women in my life, but I don't go around using them. And," he added with a dramatic pause, "I don't walk out on them."

"Well, then, who's Natasha?" Pamela countered.

Rob's nostrils flared. "Natasha? For God's sake! Natasha is a Persian cat!"

Pamela flinched, and her cheeks heated with embarrassment. It was true that she had no grounds for her accusations. It was just her own insecurity fired by idle gossip she'd overheard about Rob's love life. Nothing in his behavior toward her justified such a suspicion. She opened her mouth to stammer an apology, but Rob cut her off.

"Second, my grants have already come in for next year and, as you know, they're not from the Harley Rutherford Foundation. In fact, I've been careful not to apply to your organization. So, actually, if you think about it," he said, pointing a tanned finger at her chest, "my relationship with *you* may be costing *me* money."

Pamela nodded mutely. Of course, how could she be so dumb? He was right again. She reached out to him, but Rob was far too wound up to notice.

"Next," he went on, "I want to tell you that I'm sick and tired of hearing you put yourself down." He punctuated his statement with a jabbing motion. "Isn't it about time you gave up this childish complaining about how dull you are? You've got some sort of ridiculous inferiority complex that you've never outgrown. You're anything but a dull woman." He paused to let this thought sink in, and then continued, "Boring people don't succeed as you have or do creative things. Come on, how many people would go off and play gypsy at a Renaissance festival for six weeks?"

Pamela stared at him in confusion. She wanted so

much to believe him, but she was still filled with doubts. "I was at the festival because my life was getting to be so routine," she tried to point out.

But Rob wasn't ready to stop and listen to her. For weeks he had been pursuing this woman, but instead of the mature, adult relationship he'd hoped for, it was turning into a game of hide and seek. No sooner did he think that he and Pamela had found each other, than she'd disappear again. And he was forever "it"—the person who had to do the seeking. Well, he was getting pretty tired of this little game.

With his hands clenched on his hips, he addressed her in uncompromising tones. "Pamela," he said, "we've been lovers and we've shared the most intimate moments. But just when I'm beginning to think you care for me, you fly off like some will-o'-the-wisp. Well, I care very much about you, but I'm getting a little sick of reaching for something that keeps dissolving in my hands." He opened his fingers and spread them to show how empty they were. "I'm not going to pursue you any more. I think you'd better decide how you feel about me, and when you do decide, you'll know where to find me." Then pulling out his wallet, he took one of his business cards and slapped it on the table. While Pamela stared down at the small, white rectangle, he turned on his heel and left.

Pamela jumped. The door closing behind him sounded like a prison gate clanging shut. "Now you've done it," she scolded herself aloud as tears sprang to her eyes. Her headache had returned, and she sank down into a chair. What had she done? Distractedly she rubbed at a stain from the spilled coffee with her finger. How, Pamela wondered, could she have gone in the space of a few hours from a woman confidently in love to an abandoned mistress? Slowly, she sifted through the tangled skein of the evening's events.

Okay, she'd been nervous all along about entering

Rob's world, so she'd been unusually anxious at Reed's house. Involuntarily, her stomach knotted as she thought about how poorly she'd handled herself there. Normally she did a lot better in groups than she had tonight.

Dazedly Pamela got up, placed the mugs in the sink and ran hot water. Squirting in the liquid detergent, she ran her hands through the soapy liquid to stir up the bubbles, but her eyes hardly saw what she was doing. Events sometimes turn on such silly things, she thought. The fact that she'd worn the wrong dress had really gotten things off to a bad beginning. She'd blamed that on Rob. But was that really fair? she asked herself now. After all, he couldn't be expected to be an expert on women's fashion. Anyhow, if she'd been acting like herself, the dress wouldn't have thrown her so off-balance. She might have felt self-conscious at the start, but eventually she would have gotten over that.

Even a roomful of people in outlandish getups, she acknowledged, wouldn't ordinarily upset her. In her role as grants administrator, she'd socialized with theater people, some every bit as flamboyant as those at Reed's party, but she'd never been as judgmental of them nor as unconfident of herself as she'd been this evening. But it seemed as if tonight she'd been looking for things that would set her and Rob apart.

She thought then of how he'd gotten caught up in reminiscing with his friends. She had resented it then, but now as she considered it, she realized that it was a perfectly normal thing for him to have done. Maybe she'd just been jealous, thinking of all those years and all those experiences they'd had with him that she never would. That was really the basic problem. She could never fully participate in his world, and because of that, she couldn't really believe that their relationship would endure.

Sighing, Pamela wiped the last mug and placed it on

the shelf. Maybe what had happened tonight was for the best, she decided, trying to console herself. But she certainly didn't believe that right now. She felt like a victim of a disaster—one that she herself had caused.

Monday evening the phone rang, and Pamela reached for it with a lurching heart. Ever since her stormy parting with Rob, she had leapt at the receiver whenever someone called. It had never been Rob, though. And it wasn't this time either. It was Jake.

"Pamela?" he said, in a tentative voice, "are you okay?"

"Yes," she lied, slumping into a chair next to the wall phone in the kitchen.

"I gathered from the look on Rob's face this afternoon that things didn't go well on Friday night after I left."

Pamela straightened up. "Oh?" she said, hoping to elicit more information.

"We were in a strategy meeting this morning, and he looked like he'd had a run-in with a thunder cloud. When I tried to talk to him afterward he brushed me off."

Pamela was silent. Perversely, she found herself comforted by Jake's report.

Her friend went on. "I'm really sorry about this misunderstanding. Is there anything you'd like me to do to help straighten out this mess?"

Pamela thought for a moment. Realistically, what could he do? Perhaps Rob's jealousy of Jake had helped provoke their argument, but that wasn't really the problem. "No," she finally told Jake. "I don't think so, but thanks for the offer."

He sounded genuinely regretful. "Okay, but please remember I'm only a call away if you need me."

"Thanks, Jake. You're a true friend."

When she hung up, she sat there for a few minutes,

feeling emptier than ever. Though she was touched by Jake's offer, she couldn't imagine asking him to intercede for her. For now, she would let things ride.

However, in the following days, she found that Rob was constantly on her mind. She'd open an exciting mystery novel, only to find herself reading the same page over and over again, not comprehending a word of the text. In the office, a grant proposal for a television project would set her to imagining how Rob would portray the main role. In bed at night she'd close her eyes and his face would crowd out the rest of her dreams. At last, she felt she had to talk to someone.

Late one afternoon, over drinks at the Vista Hotel's plush lounge, she unburdened herself to Sheilah. They were sipping gin and tonics and listening to a trio of classical musicians holding forth on an indoor balcony overlooking the hotel's dramatic, many-storied lobby. At Pamela's request, Sheilah had agreed to meet her after work and now they sat among other Washington professionals and visitors to the city, soaking up the luxurious atmosphere.

"Okay," the attractive blonde said in a no-nonsense voice, "let's have it. Two weeks ago you were as starry-eyed as a teenager in love. Now you look like Camille gasping out her last breath. What's happened?"

Looking down into her drink, Pamela explained the events of the last few days as her friend leaned over the round cocktail table. When she finished her halting narrative, she gazed up to find Sheilah looking impatient.

"Pamela, are you crazy? Sounds like you had Mr. Wonderful on a string and instead of tying him up, you broke the cord and let him get away. No," she said, taking a large swallow, "I take that back. You literally cut him adrift."

Pamela went pale. Though deep down she knew her

friend was right, she defended herself anyway. "It just wasn't meant to be."

"Not meant to be!" Sheilah snorted. "I think it's time to ask yourself what you really want. Are you in love with this man?"

Pamela didn't want to say the words out loud; instead she nodded.

"I thought so. Then why are you sabotaging everything? You know what you remind me of?"

Pamela shook her head and braced herself. Sheilah could be blunt.

"You're like one of those people who won't join any club that will have them. They long to be part of things, but as soon as they're asked, they run away. Sounds to me like you've been incredibly lucky—catching this hunk's fancy—and then you go and toss him away!" The lawyer swept her hand across the table.

"What is it, Pamela? Are you afraid to commit yourself to a relationship? This isn't the first time you've driven off a really interesting man. There was that lobbyist who was crazy about you. And then there was the engineer. Boy, was he sexy." Sheilah's eyes went dreamy. "If only he had looked my way."

Pamela blanched. Sheilah's question about commitment wasn't one she'd asked herself before, but it hit a nerve. It was certainly true that none of her relationships with men ever seemed to work out. There was always something wrong—the chemistry never seemed to be quite right. "I just haven't met the perfect man," she defended herself aloud.

Sheilah gave her a straight look. "Do you really want to meet the right man?"

"What do you mean?"

"I mean that despite your little adventure at the Renaissance Festival, you're quite comfortable where you are—you've got a nice townhouse, a good job, and all the little routines that you've established for yourself over the years. Marriage or even a serious relationship with a man would threaten all that."

Pamela shot her friend a scathing look. "Are you saying that I should give up everything I've worked for all these years for a man?"

"Of course not. I'm not saying that at all," Sheilah countered, putting her drink down. "But let's be practical about this. Any good relationship involves compromise—both on your part and his—whoever he may be, if there ever is a he."

Pamela avoided Sheilah's penetrating green eyes and fumbled with her swizzle stick. She couldn't deny what her friend had said, but she really didn't want to deal with it either.

"For instance," the blonde went on, "you complained about that party Rob took you to. You felt you weren't accepted and that no one wanted to talk to you. But it really doesn't sound like you made much of an effort to accept his friends for who they were, or that you even tried to talk to them either."

A jab of recognition made Pamela flinch, but she rallied. "I could never fit in with those types of people."

"Rob wasn't asking you to become one of them. He was only asking you to spend a few hours in what you'll have to admit was a pretty interesting crowd. Believe me," the lawyer said, leaning over and tapping Pamela's arm, "I'd much rather party with a group of theater people in feathers and Indian headbands, than with a bunch of my stuffy colleagues in pinstripe suits. They may all be doing the same bit of self-promoting, but at least with your boyfriend's crowd, the scenery's more interesting."

Pamela smiled weakly. "I suppose you're right about that."

"Yeah, and I'll bet I'm right about some other things," Sheilah said as she finished her drink and swirled the ice cubes in the bottom of the heavy tumbler. She signaled the waiter for a second drink and looked inquiringly at her friend.

Pamela shook her head. She'd barely touched the first drink. Her nerves seemed to be jumping like Mexican beans. She had no idea what Sheilah was about to say next, but Pamela was sure she didn't want to hear it.

"Look," the other woman declared, as the waiter went off to get her refill, "you're not so unusual. A lot of career women, and men as well, have this kind of problem. Once you reach a certain age and have established a lifestyle, it's scary to think about making major changes. Do you remember Brad?"

"Of course," Pamela answered. Brad had been a career diplomat who'd lived with Sheilah for a year and had been crazy about her. But their torrid affair ended when Brad asked Sheilah to marry him and leave for a U.S. embassy in South America. Her friend had agonized over the issue, but had been unwilling to make the sacrifice; her lover had refused to compromise as well.

"Well," Sheilah said, taking the refill from the waiter, "I wouldn't give up everything for Brad and he couldn't give up his career for me. And we were unwilling to even work out a middle ground. I often regret that both of us were so stubborn. Perhaps if we had sat down and talked, we could have negotiated." Sheilah took a long swallow of her drink.

Pamela studied the blonde's attractive features. The set expression on the lawyer's face made Pamela realize how upsetting losing Brad had been. Even though Sheilah had ranted and raved about the whole affair when it occurred, she'd never really let on how much it still hurt her.

In an attempt to lighten her friend's mood, Pamela smiled and said, "You're becoming quite an amateur psychologist."

"We lawyers have to be. And," Sheilah said, taking

another sip of the gin and tonic, "as long as I've got you on 'my couch,' I've one more thing to say."

Once again Pamela steeled herself.

"Maybe there's no one reason why you're so afraid to commit yourself. There are probably a whole bunch of reasons. And I think one good one might be that you're afraid you'll make all these adjustments in your life and then he'll up and leave you. Isn't that what happened with your dad in a way?" she continued, referring to Thomas Stewart's early death.

Pamela's reaction was immediate. "That's pretty farfetched, isn't it?" she shot back. "Rob's nothing like my father. What's that got to do with all this anyhow?" For the first time she glared at her friend.

Sheilah shrugged. "Do we ever outgrow our childhoods? Look, we grew up together and I know that yours was pretty insecure," she pointed out, giving Pamela's hand a little squeeze. "When your father passed away your world was shattered."

Tears began to burn behind Pamela's eyes. She had felt abandoned and insecure when her father died, and she supposed that was one of the reasons why she'd lived such a careful existence. She needed the anchor of a secure lifestyle. She'd never been comfortable taking risks—particularly with male-female relationships. The Renaissance Festival had been a big step for her. But Robert Darcy, with his spontaneity, natural curiosity and openness to life's possibilities, represented a giant leap across a bottomless chasm. Though she was in love with him, his mercurial nature threatened her safe little world.

"You've admitted that you love this guy," Sheilah said, interrupting Pamela's thoughts. "Have you told him that?"

"No," Pamela admitted. She hadn't had the courage. Even that night at her apartment when he'd told her of his feelings, she'd kept silent.

"Well, for God's sake, Pamela. Live dangerously. Tell him how it is with you."

"Telling him how I feel won't solve all our problems," Pamela said thoughtfully.

"Maybe not. But at least it will be a step in the right direction." Sheilah took a last sip of her drink and looked at her watch. "I've got to run." She pulled out her wallet and put several bills on the table. "My treat."

Then standing up, the tall blonde leaned over and patted Pamela on the shoulder. "Look, I've been a bit tough on you tonight. But do consider what I said. I hate to think of you sitting around having regrets about Rob the way I still do about Brad."

A moment later, Sheilah was gone and Pamela sat alone at the table. She knew she should leave as well, but her mind was so filled with whirling thoughts that she lingered, trying to sort them out. Many things that Sheilah had said struck home. And she knew she had some serious thinking to do.

10

Pamela sat staring at the silent phone. She'd always deplored the idea of women hanging over a telephone, praying that some elusive man would call. But here she was, wishing that Rob would contact her, even though she knew it was hopeless. He wasn't going to call; he was going to wait until she made the first move.

And she'd been trying to do that for the past week, but every time she lifted the receiver, she lost her nerve. Several times, she'd gotten as far as dialing the number, but then she'd put down the phone on the first ring.

She was beginning to hate her own wishy-washiness. This couldn't go on any longer. She had to get things settled with Rob, one way or the other. If she didn't, she'd wake up some morning, a bitter old woman with an empty life.

Decisively, she picked up the telephone one more time and called his number at home. As the phone rang she could hear her heart beating, and when someone answered on the other end, her fingers clenched the receiver so tightly, the knuckles had turned white. Rob said "Hello" and taking a deep breath, she began to launch into a breathless apology. But she said no more than two or three words before she realized he was still talking. "I'm sorry I can't come to the phone right now," his cultivated baritone went on. Pamela released her breath in a long sigh. It was a recorded message on his answering machine. There was no way she was going to leave her name on a tape recorder.

Quickly, she put down the receiver and sat back in the chair staring at the phone in frustration. She'd just have to try later, and she knew that now she would. But though she called several times that evening, Rob was never at home. By the next day, Saturday, she was almost frantic to speak to him, but she wouldn't disturb him before ten—he might be sleeping late—alone, she hoped.

That morning, as she was scrambling some eggs for breakfast, she heard the sound of letters slipping through the mail slot in her front door. While the eggs bubbled on the stove, she padded out to the front hall and picked up an unusually large collection of circulars, catalogues and envelopes. As she sorted through the stack, she stopped short. One of the letters bore the imprint of The Folger Library in its upper left-hand corner. Quickly, she tore the envelope open. However, in the next second, the smell of burning eggs sent her running to the range to turn off the gas. Removing the skillet from the burner, she flopped the eggs into a plate and then turned back to the mysterious letter. When she shook it upside down, a ticket to the opening performance of *The Tempest* tumbled out.

Pamela's eyes lit up. It must be from Rob. So he hadn't forgotten her, she thought, putting a hand to her breast. Only yesterday, she'd seen the ad for the play in the paper and knew that he was starring in the role of

Prospero. The date on the ticket was for that evening. All at once, Pamela felt as though she'd been given a shot of Adrenalin. Suddenly there seemed to be a million things that needed doing to ready herself for the evening, and magically, she had more than enough energy for all of them.

The first thing she did was call her hairdresser, who agreed to squeeze her in. Then, after gulping down her coffee and the singed eggs, she rushed upstairs to take a cursory glance at her closet. Nothing in it seemed special enough. She'd have to buy a new dress.

That evening, Pamela stood in front of the mirror, inspecting the results of her day of preparation. She looked good, she had to admit, turning from side to side and admiring the spring green two-piece dress she'd found in a boutique on Connecticut Avenue. Tilting her head, she looked approvingly at the rich waves of honey brown spilling down her back. She'd had Raphael do her hair long and loose, the way Rob liked it.

With an excited step, she picked up her handbag and a light wrap. Within minutes, she was in her little compact car heading over to the Folger.

An hour later, Pamela sat entranced watching the first act of Shakespeare's most moving comedy, her emotions churning inside her. She was terribly proud of Rob, who played his role of the enchanted island's aging magician with great finesse and power. She'd known, after a summer of watching him delight audiences as Robyn O'Dare, that he was a gifted actor. But now, as he moved across the stage, dominating it entirely with his dramatic presence, she realized the magnitude of his talent. How could she have ever thought Rob was merely a vagabond player who lived from moment to moment? It was obvious that he was not only serious about his craft, but dedicated to it. His ability to interpret the subtle and profound nature of Prospero forced her to acknowledge that Rob's own emotional nature ran very deep indeed. Surely, this was a man who didn't just live on the surface of life but who was fully capable of making a commitment. If only that commitment could be to her.

When the play ended and Rob took his final bows, Pamela clapped louder than anyone else in the Folger's intimate Elizabethan theater. So moving had been his performance that she wanted to shout "bravo" and stand on her seat. Not quite having the nerve to do that, she settled for looking up at him with her heart in her eyes. She wasn't sure he had seen her in the darkened house, but he must know she was there, since he'd sent her the tickets.

As the audience began to file out, Pamela stayed in her seat, wondering how to get back to the actor's dressing room. Finally she asked an usher, who directed her to the rear of the stage. As she climbed up the steps and headed toward the side curtains, she noticed that several of the performers had congregated in the wings to chat with each other and with friends who'd come backstage to congratulate them.

Rob in his long wizard's robe was busy talking to the pretty brunette actress who'd played his daughter. Absorbed in the conversation, he didn't notice Pamela's approach. When she stopped within a few feet of him, he didn't look up. She stood there, a big expectant smile on her face, clutching the program as she waited for him to see her. When he finally did glance her way, however, the startled expression on his face gave her a twinge of alarm. He didn't look like a man who had been expecting a reunion with his estranged lover. For a moment they stared at each other, and the pretty, young actress, taking note of the sudden tension in the air, excused herself and backed away.

"Pamela," Rob blurted out. "What in the world are you doing here?"

"I . . . that is, when I got the ticket you sent . . ." Pamela stammered.

Rob looked blank. "Ticket?"

Confusion clouded her delicate features. Then, suddenly she realized that she'd made a mistake. "I thought, that is, I got a ticket in the mail and I assumed, umm, that you'd sent it."

Just at that moment, Jake rushed over to them. "Pamela," he cried, shooting her a broad grin, "I'm so glad you made it. How did you like Rob here?" He put a hand on the taller man's shoulder. "Laurence Olivier, eat your heart out!"

Pamela tried to respond with a laugh, but even to her own ears, it sounded forced. Clearly, it had been Jake who'd sent her the ticket—probably in a misguided effort to get her and Rob back together again. But the disconcerted expression on Rob's face made her think he wasn't eager for that to happen. Very possibly, she thought, he already had a date with the attractive young woman he'd been talking to before. The only way to deal with the awkward situation was to leave.

Turning to her benefactor, she squeezed his hand and said, "I really enjoyed the play, Jake. Thank you so much for sending me the ticket." She looked back at Rob without quite meeting his eyes, offered him congratulations with the brightest smile she could muster and pleaded a long day. Then excusing herself, she left the two mystified men staring after her as she exited the stage and made her way hastily up the flagstone aisle.

Even as she climbed into her car, Pamela trembled with mortification. Why hadn't she thought that it might be Jake and not Rob who'd sent the ticket? She felt like a serving girl who'd dared approach the king and had been sent packing to the kitchens. What a disaster this had been.

Her disappointment and embarrassment had only deepened by the time she'd returned to her townhouse. When she'd set off that evening, her expectations had been so high; now they'd fallen back to earth with a jolting crash. Running up the stairs to her bedroom, she slammed the door shut, flicked on the light and kicked off the beige pumps she'd purchased that afternoon to go with her new dress. In a moment, the dress followed the shoes to the floor. Never would she ever wear that dress again in her life, she told herself as she stomped into the bathroom.

Pulling her hair away from her forehead, she looked into the mirror and frowned. Now all her carefully applied makeup seemed phony—as if she'd put it on to audition for a part that she hadn't won. Grabbing a washcloth, she dampened it and vigorously scrubbed her face as though to erase the disconcerting memories of the evening.

But when she surveyed her squeaky clean image, it was with a growing feeling of depression. Her skin was red from her abrasive attack with the washcloth. Her eyes, on the other hand, were red from an entirely different cause. She looked like someone who was about to cry and that was the way she felt.

"How could you be so stupid," she said to the reflection. But it had no answer, and she finally turned away, her shoulders drooping. Forlornly, she pulled open her dresser drawer and reached in for a night-gown. Her hand brought up a filmy aqua gown that had been a Christmas present from a favorite, ever hopeful aunt. It seemed so absurd to wear such a sexy garment on a night like this, but she didn't have the energy to put it back. So, without paying any further attention to it, she hauled the sheer fabric over her head and pulled it down over her hips. Then she walked over to the bed and sat with her head propped against the pillow.

But after she turned the light off, she didn't bother to get in underneath the covers. Instead, she stared at the pattern of moonlight on her rose-colored coverlet. She was far too disturbed to fall asleep, and she realized she'd probably be sitting there half the night with her eyes wide open. Her cheeks burned as she replayed the evening's scene in her head. She'd felt like such a fool, and she certainly must have seemed like one to him. She hadn't handled the situation with Jake very well either. She'd just made him feel awkward about his gift and his good intentions. Shaking her head, she clenched her fingers so tightly that she unconsciously dug her nails into the flesh of her palms.

At that moment, a rap at her bedroom window made her jump, sending her thoughts scattering. Quickly, her eyes went to the second-story balcony window. Squinting, she could barely make out a dark figure standing on the other side, tapping against the glass. Her hand flew to her mouth in fear, and her heart began beating wildly. She'd been meaning to buy a charley bar for months, but she hadn't gotten around to it. Even though there hadn't been any break-ins in her neighborhood recently, she was well aware that Washington, like all cities, had a high crime rate. A woman living alone was an easy target.

Edging quietly toward the phone, Pamela lifted the receiver to call the police. However, as her finger hit the first digit of the emergency number, she stopped short. The balcony door had slid open and the dark figure on the other side was entering her bedroom. Frantically, Pamela reached for something to use as a weapon.

Just as her hand closed around her hairbrush, she heard a familiar voice quip, "I'm getting much too old for this sort of Romeo thing." It was Rob.

Breathing a sigh of relief, she let go of the hairbrush

and stared at him. "Rob! What in the world? . . . What are you trying to do? Give me a heart attack?"

"Yes," he said, holding out his arms and moving toward her with a confident stride. "Only not the medical kind."

Guiding her gently back down on the bed, he sat next to her and took her by the shoulders. "I climbed up your balcony because you refused to answer your front door."

"Refused? Oh," she said, looking at the shut bedroom door, "I guess I just didn't hear the bell."

Rob squeezed her shoulders. "I'm glad to know that. Just when I'd gotten my hopes up, I was afraid you might still be shutting me out."

"Oh, Rob. That will never happen again." She touched his cheek.

His voice was husky. "Pamela, I didn't send you that ticket, but I wish I had."

"You do?" She looked inquiringly into his shadowy face.

"Yes, and I'm sorry I wasn't more welcoming when you came backstage. I was just so stunned to see you." He reached over and switched on the bedside lamp which flooded the room with its soft illumination. When he could see her more clearly, his eyes were drawn to the soft, gauzy folds of her gown. Slowly his eyebrows began to rise. "You looked beautiful tonight in that green thing you wore, but now," he said, his gaze sweeping appreciatively over her tantalizingly revealed body, "you're absolutely gorgeous."

A self-conscious protest rose in her throat, but she stopped it mid-sentence. Why not just accept the wonderful things Rob said? she asked herself.

"I know our matchmaking friend Jake sent you the ticket. But why did you come?" Rob demanded.

Now was the time to be honest, Pamela realized. "Because I missed you and I wanted to tell you so. I wanted to tell you that I love you."

"Oh, Pamela," he said, pulling her against his hard chest, "I adore you."

"I've been so stupid," Pamela murmured into the folds of his shirt.

"That makes two of us. Let's make a pact." Pamela lifted her head. "Let's not be stupid anymore."

"What do you mean?"

"I mean we've let our differences get in the way. Instead, let's capitalize on them, and not use them to divide us from one another."

He wasn't really talking about himself, she realized. From the first, she'd been the one who'd magnified every little dissimilarity between them into a gigantic chasm. "Oh, Rob," she finally exclaimed, "I know now how foolish it was of me to let my insecurities keep us apart."

Tenderly, he placed a finger to her lips to hold back her regretful words. "No more apologies. From now on we look forward to a future together. We won't worry about the past."

Pamela looked up at him quizzically. What did he mean by "a future"? she wondered.

Rob answered that unspoken question with his next words. "Remember the poem I quoted to you the first time we made love?"

She blinked. "'A Valediction Forbidding Mourning?'"

He nodded. "That's the one. I'd asked you to think about it. Have you?"

Slowly, she shook her head and Rob clucked his tongue. "A fine student you are," he teased. But then his expression grew more serious as he began to quote the famous love poem.

"If they be two, they are two so
As stiffe twin compasses are two,
Thy soule the fixt foot, makes no show
To move, but doth, if the 'other doe."

When he finished, he looked inquiringly at her. "Do you understand now?"

"Donne," she said, feeling a bit like a college student talking to a professor, "is comparing their relationship to a twin compass—the kind of thing I used to make circles with in geometry in high school."

"Yes. The two parts of the compass play different roles. One arm stays put while the other travels around it. Yet the fact is that each part requires the other for harmony."

"Are you saying that we're that way?"

"I think we could be and I hope that we will be. You, with your quiet, thoughtful nature, are the anchor—the person who gives stability to us as a couple. Without you, Pamela, frankly, I feel lost. I'd zigzag in useless patterns, but with you at my side, no matter what new challenges I take on, I'll go in the right direction."

Now at last Pamela was really beginning to understand his meaning. "And as long as I'm with you, I'll be challenged."

"Sounds like we're a team. Maybe one that should be together permanently," he said, drawing her even closer and lowering his head to hers. "Oh, Pamela, don't you realize how much I love you? I think I fell in love with you that first day we met. I'll never forget the way you looked when I turned and found you staring up at me when I trampled your rum cakes. And I'll never forget that kiss." With that, he claimed her lips with his again.

Their first kiss had been devastating and dramatic,

but this one was the sweetest that Pamela had ever known. And as she succumbed to its seduction, she wrapped her arms tightly around Rob's neck and clung to him. From now on, he would be hers, and she, his. Their differences would only make their union of heart and mind stronger. But as Rob reached across to switch off the light, it was the union of their bodies they ached for as well.

Epilogue

Pamela spread out the last box of rum cakes and surveyed the effect. Unlike the previous summer's searing temperatures, the weather this year was seasonably pleasant. The clear skies and crisp September air had drawn large crowds to this first day of the fair, and Pamela was expecting to make even more of a profit on her pastries and cider than she had before.

"How are you feeling?" Tess shouted from across the way. "You look great!"

"I feel that way," Pamela called back. And it was the truth. She felt absolutely wonderful, and being back with all her old friends at the Renaissance Festival only added to her exhilaration and contentment.

She was just bending over to get some napkins from the shelves below the counter, when a flying red object caught the corner of her eye.

"Jake!" she shouted, straightening awkwardly to greet the jaunty figure juggling apples in front of her.

"Pamela, my love," he said, leaning over the edge of the stand and giving her a kiss. "You look radiant."

"Life is treating me pretty well," she agreed, running a hand through her rich mane of wavy brown hair.

Just then the sound of a baritone voice distracted both her and Jake.

"Thou villainous saltpetre! Thou spoonful of brains!"

"Oh, dear," Pamela exclaimed, glancing up to see a handsome dark-haired gallant crossing swords with a redheaded opponent. As the two swashbucklers danced in battle, they were edging steadily toward her booth. Quickly, Pamela began to gather up her rum cakes. But her frantic efforts were too late. Suddenly the handsome raven-haired swordsman rushed up the incline to her stand and vaulted over it with easy grace.

Grinning from ear to ear, he seized Pamela in his powerful arms and kissed her soundly, much to the amusement of the crowd following close behind. "A kiss for my beauteous wife who makes the best rum cakes in town. And a 'hi ho' to our little one," he added, patting Pamela gently on her rounded stomach. The crowd cheered as he kissed her once more. Then, stealing a rum cake, he once again leapt over her counter and resumed his mock battle.

As he disappeared into the throng, Pamela turned to Jake the Jester with a playful scowl. "Milord, pray who was that insolent varlet?"

"'Twas Robyn O'Dare, who has stolen many a kiss," the jester exclaimed. "But you, Fair Lady, are the only damsel to have captured his heart."

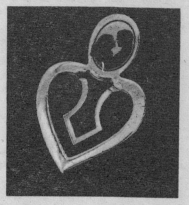

ANNE MATHER

Anne Mather, one of Harlequin's leading romance authors, has published more than 100 million copies worldwide, including **Wild Concerto**, a *New York Times* best-seller.

Catherine Loring was an innocent in a South American country beset by civil war. Doctor Armand Alvares was arrogant yet compassionate. They could not ignore the flame of love igniting within them...whatever the cost.

At your favorite bookstore in June.

HIF-B-I

HIDDEN IN THE FLAME